The Pony Rider Boys in New Mexico; Or, The End of the Silver Trail

by
Frank Gee Patchin

The Pony Rider Boys in New Mexico; Or, The End of the Silver Trail
by Frank Gee Patchin

Copyright © 2023

All Rights reserved.
No part of this publication may be reproduced, stored in a retrieval system, or transmitted in any form or by any means, electronic, mechanical, photocopying or Otherwise, without the written permission of the publisher.

The author/editor asserts the moral right to be identified as the author/editor of this work.

ISBN: 978-93-57484-18-3

Published by
DOUBLE 9 BOOKS

2/13-B, Ansari Road
Daryaganj, New Delhi – 110002
info@double9books.com
www.double9books.com
Tel. 011-40042856

This book is under public domain

ABOUT THE AUTHOR

Frank Gee Patchin (1861-1925) was born in Wayland, New York, United States. was an American writer of children's books. He is known for his famous Battleship Boy series and his Pony Rider Boys series, which have many readers today as well. Patchin has published more than 200 adventure books. Most of them were published under the pen names of Victor Durham and Jessie Graham Flower. He has also written for the Edward Stratemeyer Syndicate.

CONTENTS

CHAPTER I.
SOMETHING IN THE WIND 7

CHAPTER II.
IN THE ZUNI FOOTHILLS 16

CHAPTER III.
INDIANS! 21

CHAPTER IV.
ON THE TRAIL OF JUAN 28

CHAPTER V.
A DARING ACT 35

CHAPTER VI.
THE FIRE DANCE OF THE RED MEN 40

CHAPTER VII.
FLEEING FROM THE ENEMY 49

CHAPTER VIII.
ASLEEP ON THE SLEEPY GRASS 56

CHAPTER IX.
THE MIDNIGHT ALARM 61

CHAPTER X.
MEETING THE ATTACK 68

CHAPTER XI.
RIDING WITH KRIS KRINGLE 75

CHAPTER XII.
THE DASH FOR LIFE 83

CHAPTER XIII.
FOLLOWING A HOT TRAIL 89

CHAPTER XIV.
   AGAINST BIG ODDS 95
CHAPTER XV.
   HIT BY A DRY STORM 102
CHAPTER XVI.
   CHUNKY'S NEW IDEA 110
CHAPTER XVII.
   IN THE HOME OF THE CAVE DWELLERS 115
CHAPTER XVIII.
   FACING THE ENEMY'S GUNS 122
CHAPTER XIX.
   OUTWITTING THE REDSKINS 128
CHAPTER XX.
   TILTING FOR THE SILVER SPURS 134
CHAPTER XXI.
   THE FAT BOY'S DISCOVERY 140
CHAPTER XXII.
   IN HAND-TO-HAND CONFLICT 146
CHAPTER XXIII.
   MOONBEAM POINTS THE WAY 151
CHAPTER XXIV.
   CONCLUSION 161

CHAPTER I.
SOMETHING IN THE WIND

"What was that?"

"Only one of the boys in the seat behind us, snoring."

"Sure they're asleep?"

"Yes, but what if they're not? They are only kids. They wouldn't understand."

"Don't you be too sure about that. I've heard about those kids. Heard about 'em over in Nevada. There's four of them. They call themselves the Pony Rider Boys; and they're no tenderfeet, if all I hear is true. They have done some pretty lively stunts."

"Yes, that's all right, Bob, but we ain't going to begin by getting cold feet over a bunch of kids out for a holiday."

"Where they going?"

"Don't know. Presume they'll be taking a trip over the plains or heading for the mountains. They've got a stock car up ahead jammed full of stock and equipment."

"Scarecrows?"

"No. Good stock. Some of the slickest ponies you ever set eyes on. There's one roan there that I wouldn't mind owning. Maybe we can make a trade," and the speaker chuckled softly to himself.

A snore louder than those that had preceded it, caused the two men to laugh heartily.

The snore had come from Stacy Brown. Both he and Tad Butler were resting from their long journey on the Atlantic and Pacific train. Further to the rear of the car, their companions, Ned Rector and Walter Perkins, also were curled up in a double seat, with Professor Zepplin sitting very straight as if sleep were furthest from his thoughts. They were nearing their destination now, and within the hour would be unloading their stock and equipment at Bluewater.

"They're asleep all right," grinned one of the two men who occupied the seat just ahead of Stacy and Tad. "Is old man Marquand going to meet us at the station?"

"Oh, no. That wouldn't be a good thing. Might attract too much attention. Told him not to. We'll get a couple of ponies at Bluewater and ride across the mountains. But we've got to be slick. The old man is no fool. He'll hang on to the location of the treasure till the last old cat's gone to sleep for good."

"Any idea where the place is?"

"No. Except that it's somewhere south of the Zuni range."

A solitary eye in the seat behind, opened cautiously. The eye belonged to Stacy Brown. The last snore had awakened him, and he had lain with closed eyes listening to the conversation of the two men.

He gave Tad a gentle nudge, which was returned with a soft pressure on Stacy's right arm as a warning that he was to remain quiet.

"Do you know what the treasure consists of?"

"Maybe a mine, but as near as I could draw from Marquand's talk it is jewels and Spanish money which one of the old Franciscan monks had buried. The Pueblos knew where it was, but they sealed the place up after the Pueblo revolution in 1680, and it's been corked tight ever since."

"How'd Marquand get wise to it?"

"From an old Pueblo Chief whose life he saved a few months ago. The old chief died a little while afterwards, but before he went, he told Marquand about the treasure."

"Didn't suppose a redskin had so much gratitude under his tough skin. Does the old man know where the place is?"

"No, not exactly. That's where we come in," grinned the speaker. "We are going to help him find it."

"And then?"

"Oh, well. There's lots of ways to get rid of him."

"You mean?"

"He might tumble off into a canyon, or something of the sort, in the night time. Here's the place."

The train was rounding a bend into the little town of Bluewater.

"Sit still," whispered Tad. "I want to get a look at those fellows so I'll know them next time I see them."

The Pony Rider boy left his seat, and hurrying to the forward end of the car, helped himself to a drink of water from the tank; then slowly retraced his steps.

As he walked down the car, he took in the two men in one swift, comprehensive glance, then swung his hands to his companions at the other end of the car, as a signal that they were arriving at their destination.

"Know 'em?" whispered Stacy as Tad began pulling his baggage from the rack.

"Never saw either before. Better get your stuff together. This train is fast only when it stops. It drags along over the country, but when it gets into a station it's always in a hurry to get away," laughed Tad.

A few minutes later the party of bronzed young men sprang from the car to the station platform, where they instantly became the center of a throng of curious villagers.

Readers of the preceding volumes of this series are already too well acquainted with the Pony Rider Boys to need a formal introduction. As told in "THE PONY RIDER BOYS IN THE ROCKIES," the lads had set out from their homes in Missouri for a summer's vacation in the saddle. That first volume detailed how the lads penetrated the fastnesses of the Rockies, hunted big game and how they finally discovered the Lost Claim, which they won after fighting a battle with the mountaineers, thus earning for themselves quite a fortune.

In "THE PONY RIDER BOYS IN TEXAS," the boys were again seen to advantage. There they joined in a cattle drive across the state as cowboys. They played an exciting part in the rough life of the cowmen, meeting with many stirring adventures. It will be remembered how, in this story, Tad Butler saved a large part of the herd, besides performing numerous heroic deeds, including the saving of the life of a member of the party from a swollen river. At the end of their journey, they solved a deep mystery—a mystery that had perplexed and worried the cattle men, besides causing them heavy financial loss.

In "THE PONY RIDER BOYS IN MONTANA," the scene shifted to the old Custer Trail, the battle ground of one of the most tragic events in American history. The story described how Tad Butler overheard a plot to stampede and kill a flock of many thousand sheep; how after experiencing many hardships, he finally carried the news to the owner of the herd; then later, participated in the battle between the cowmen and sheep herders, in which the latter emerged victorious.

It will be recalled too, how the Pony Rider Boy was captured by the Blackfeet Indians and taken to their mountain retreat, where with a young companion he was held until they made their escape with the assistance of an Indian maiden; how they were pursued by the savages, the bullets from whose rifles singing over the heads of the lads as they headed for a river into which they plunged, thus effectually throwing off the savage pursuers; and finally, how in time they made their way back to the camp of the Pony Riders, having solved the mystery of the old Custer Trail.

After these exciting adventures, the lads concluded to cut short their Montana trip and go on to the next stage of their journeyings, which was destined to be even more stirring than any that had preceded it. How Tad Butler and Stacy Brown proved themselves to be real heroes, was told in "THE PONY RIDER BOYS IN THE OZARKS."

For a long time, an organized band of thieves had been stealing stock in the Ozark range, baffling all efforts to apprehend them. The boys had been warned to guard their own stock carefully, but despite this, their ponies were stolen from camp, one by one and in a most mysterious manner, until not an animal was left. Then, one by one, the Pony Rider Boys became lost until only Tad and Stacy remained. They were facing starvation, and it will be recalled how Tad Butler made a plucky trip to the nearest mining camp for assistance. There the boys were imprisoned underground by a mine explosion; escaping from which, they met with perils every bit as grave, and from which they were eventually rescued by Stacy himself.

Through the disaster, the lads solved the Secret of the Ruby Mountain, thus putting an end for good to the wholesale thieving in the Ozark range.

Though the Pony Rider Boys had suffered many hardships in their journeyings, those that lay before them were destined to try them even more. In "THE PONY RIDER BOYS IN THE ALKALI," they faced the perils of the baking alkali desert. It will be recalled how they fought desperately for water when all the usual sources of supply were found to have run dry; how Tad and Stacy Brown were captured by a desert hermit and thrown into a cave; how, after their escape, they were lost in the Desert Maze, and how after many hardships, they finally succeeded in making their way to camp, dragging behind them a wild coyote that Tad had roped when the boys were beset by the wild beasts in the dead of night.

Nothing daunted by their trying experiences the Pony Rider Boys set out on the concluding trip of the season—a journey over the historic plains and mountains of New Mexico. After a long railroad ride, they had finally arrived at the town of Bluewater, from which they were to begin their explorations in the southwest.

A guide was to meet and conduct them across the mountains of the Zuni range and so on to the southern borders of the state.

By the time they reached the platform of the station, the stock car had been uncoupled and was being shifted to a side track where they might unload their belongings at their leisure.

"I wonder where that guide is," said Tad.

"He was told to be here," answered the Professor.

"Never mind; we can unload better without him," averred Ned, starting off at a brisk trot for their car which had been shunted alongside the platform at the rear of the station.

With joyous anticipation of the new scenes and experiences that lay before them, the lads set briskly to work, and within an hour had all the stock and equipment removed from the car.

There was quite an imposing collection, with their ponies, their burros, tents and other equipment, the latter lying strewn all over the open level space beyond the station.

"Looks as if a circus had just come to town," laughed Walter.

"We've got a side show, anyway," retorted Ned.

"What's our side show?"

"Chunky's that."

"No; he's the clown. The rest of us are the animals, only we're not in cages."

"Hey, fellows, see that funny Mexican on the burro there," laughed Chunky. "Guess he never saw an outfit like ours before."

The lads could not repress a laugh as they glanced at the figure pointed out by Stacy.

The man was sitting on the burro, his feet extended on the ground before him, hands thrust deep into trousers pockets. He was observing the work of the boys curiously. The fellow's high, conical head was crowned by a peaked Mexican hat, much the worse for wear, while his coarse, black hair was combed straight down over a pair of small, piercing, dark eyes. The complexion, or such of it as was visible through the mask of wiry hair, was swarthy, his form thin and insignificant.

Stacy Brown strode over to him somewhat pompously.

"You speak English?" questioned the boy.

"Si, señor."

The Mexican's lips curled back, revealing two rows of gleaming, white teeth.

"I'm glad to hear it. I didn't think you could. We are looking for a guide who was to have met us here to conduct us over the mountains. His name is Juan. It'll be something else when he does show up. Do you know him?"

"Si, señor."

"Isn't he coming to meet us?"

"Si, señor."

"Well, I must say he's taking his time about getting here. Where is he?"

"Juan here, señor."

"Here? I don't see him," answered the lad, looking about the place.

"Me Juan," grinned the Mexican. "You?"

"Never mind the señor. I'll take for granted I'm a señor, or whatever else you think. Say, fellows, come here," commanded Stacy.

"Well, what's the matter?" demanded Ned, approaching, followed by the other boys.

"This is it," announced Stacy, with a wave of his hand toward the Mexican.

"What is it?" sniffed Ned.

"This."

"Chunky, what are you getting at?" questioned Walter.

"Perhaps this gentleman will know where we may find our guide," interrupted the Professor, coming up. "Señor, do you know one Juan—"

"Yes, he knows him," grinned Stacy. "He's very well acquainted with the gentleman."

"Then where may we find this Juan

"That's Juan—that's your guide," Stacy informed the Professor.

"You—are you the guide?"

"Si, señor."

The Professor opened his eyes in amazement. The burro, on the other hand, stood with nose to the ground sound asleep, oblivious to all that was taking place about him.

"Why didn't you make yourself known—why haven't you helped us to unload?" demanded the Professor in an irritated tone.

"Me no *peon*. Me guide."

"He's a guide," explained Stacy. "Guides don't work, you know, Professor. They are just ornaments. He and the burro are going to pose for our amusement."

The boys laughed heartily. Professor Zepplin uttered an exclamation of impatience.

"Sir, if you are going with this outfit you will be expected to do your share of the labor. There are no drones in our hive."

"No; we all work," interposed Stacy.

"And some of us are eaters," added Ned.

Juan shrugged his shoulders and showed his pearly teeth.

At the Professor's command, however, Juan stepped off the burro without in the least disturbing that animal's dreams and lazily began collecting the baggage as directed by the Professor. After the equipment had been sorted into piles, the boys did it up into neat packs which they skillfully strapped to the backs of the burros of their pack train. Juan, lost in contemplation of their labors, forgot his own duties until reminded of them by Stacy, who gave the guide a violent poke in the ribs with his thumb.

Juan started; then, with a sheepish grin, became busy again.

It was no small task to get their belongings in packs preparatory to the journey; but late in the afternoon the boys had completed their task. They had had nothing to eat since early morning. But they were too anxious to be on their way to wait for dinner in town.

After making some necessary purchases in the village, the procession finally started away across the plain.

"You'll never get anywhere with that sleepy burro, Juan," decided the Professor, with a shake of the head.

"Him go fast," grinned the Mexican.

"So can a crab on dry land," jeered Ned.

Just then the guide utter a series of shrill "yi-yi's," whereupon the lads were treated to an exhibition such as they never had seen before.

The sleepy burro projected his head straight out before him, while his tail, raised to a level with his back, stuck straight out behind him. The burro, seemingly imbued with sudden life, was off at a pace faster than a man could run.

It was most astonishing. The boys gazed in amazement; then burst out in a chorus of approving yells.

But it was the rider, even more than the burro, that excited their mirth. His long legs were working like those of a jumping jack, and though astride of the burro, Juan was walking at a lively pace. It reminded one of the way men propelled the old-fashioned velocipedes years before.

A cloud of dust rose behind the odd outfit as the party drew out on the plains. Their ponies were started at a gallop, which was necessary to enable them to keep up with the pace that Juan had set.

"Here! Here!" shouted the Professor.

Juan never looked back.

"We're leaving the pack train. Slow down!"

Laughingly the lads pulled their ponies down to a walk; then halted entirely to enable the burros to catch up with them. By this time the pack animals had become so familiar with their work that little attention was necessary on the part of the boys. Now and then one more sleepy than the rest would go to sleep and pause to doze a few minutes on the trail. This always necessitated all hands stopping to wait until the sleeper could be rounded up and driven up to the bunch.

Juan had disappeared. They were discussing the advisability of sending one of the boys out after him when he was seen returning. But at what a different gait! His burro was dragging itself along with nose to the ground, while Juan himself was slouching on its back half asleep.

"You must have a motor inside that beast," grinned Tad.

"Him go some, señor?"

"Him do," answered Stacy, his solemn eyes taking in the sleepy burro wonderingly.

"Better not waste your energy performing," advised the Professor. "We shall need what little you have. We will make camp here, as I see there is a spring near by. Help the boys unpack the burros."

"Si, señor," answered the guide, standing erect and permitting his burro to walk from under him.

With shouts and songs the lads, in great good humor, went to work at once, pitching their camp for the first time on the plains of New Mexico. There was much to be done, and twilight was upon them before they had advanced far enough to begin cooking their evening meal.

CHAPTER II.
IN THE ZUNI FOOTHILLS

A sudden wail from the guide attracted the attention of the party to him at once. "Now what's the matter?" demanded Tad, hurrying to him.

The guide had thrown himself prone upon the ground and was groaning as if in great agony, offering no reply to the question.

"Are you sick?"

"Si, si, señor," moaned Juan.

"Where?"

"Estomago—mucho malo."

"Your stomach?"

"He's got a pain under his apron," diagnosed Stacy solemnly.

"Been working too hard," suggested Ned.

In the meantime the guide was rolling and twisting on the ground, glancing appealingly from one to the other of them.

"Professor, hadn't you better fetch your medicine case and dose him up?" asked Tad.

"Yes, I'll attend to him."

"Give him a good dose while you are about it," urged Ned. "Something that will cure his laziness at the same time."

The Professor brought his case; then, remembering something else in his kit that he wanted, he laid the case down and hurried back to his tent. However, Stacy opened the case, selecting a bottle, apparently at random, drew the cork and held the bottle under Juan's nose.

"Smell of this, my son. It'll cure your estomago on the run."

"Be careful, Chunky, what are you doing there?" warned Tad. "You shouldn't fool with the medicines. You—"

His further remarks were cut short by a sudden yell of terror and pain from Juan.

The guide leaped to his feet choking, gasping, while the tears ran down his cheeks as he danced about as if suddenly bereft of his senses.

"Now you've gone and done it," growled Ned. "He never moved so fast in his life, I'll wager."

Juan was running in a circle now, shrieking and moaning. Professor Zepplin approached them in a series of leaps. He could not imagine what new disaster had overtaken the lazy Mexican.

"Here, here, here, what's the trouble now?" He demanded sternly. "Stop that howling!"

"Chunky's been prescribing for your patient in your absence," Ned informed him.

The Professor grabbed the wild guide by the collar, giving him a vigorous shake. When he released his grip, Juan sank to the ground in a heap, moaning weakly.

"What's that you say? Stacy prescribed—"

"I—I let him smell of the bottle," explained Stacy guiltily.

"What bottle?"

Stacy slowly picked up the offending bottle and handed it to the Professor.

"Ammonia! Boy, you might have put his eyes out! Never let this occur again. Remember, you are not to touch the medicines under any circumstances whatever!"

"Yes, sir," agreed Chunky meekly, while Ned Rector strolled away, shaking with laughter.

"Drink," begged the patient.

"Fetch him some water," directed Professor Zepplin.

"No, no, no, señor," protested Juan, gesticulating protestingly.

"What do you want?"

"Guess he wants something stronger than water," suggested Ned.

"Si, si, si," agreed the guide, showing his white teeth in an approving grin.

"You won't get anything stronger than that in this outfit, unless you cook yourself some coffee," muttered Tad.

"That's what's the matter with him," decided Chunky, who had been observing the sick man keenly.

"Guess we drew a prize when we got Juan," announced Walter.

"Give him some medicine, anyway," urged Ned. "He is sick— let him take the dose."

"Let him have the worst you've got in your case, Professor," added Tad, with a laugh.

A grim smile played about the corners of Professor Zepplin's mouth as he ran his fingers over the bottles in his medicine case. Finally, selecting one that seemed to fit the particular ailment of his patient, he directed Chunky to fetch a spoon.

By this time Juan was protesting volubly that he was "all better" and did not need the medicine. The Professor gave no heed to the fellow's protestations.

"Open your mouth," he commanded.

Juan shut his teeth tightly together.

"Open your mouth!" commanded the Professor sternly. "We want no sick men about this camp. It will fix you in a minute."

But the guide steadfastly refused to separate the white teeth.

"Boys, open his mouth while I pour the medicine down him," gritted the Professor.

They required no urging to do the Professor's bidding. Tad and Ned ranged themselves on either side of the patient, while Chunky sat on the guide's feet. Almost before he was aware of their purpose the boys had pried his jaws open and into the opening thus made professor Zepplin dropped the concoction he had mixed.

The effect was electrical. Juan leaped to his feet as if elevated by springs, uttering a yell that might have been heard a mile or more on the open plain. But Juan did not run in a circle this time. Acting upon the mathematical theory that a straight line is the shortest distance between two points, the guide made a break for the spring, howling like a madman. The Pony Rider Boys looked on in amazement.

Juan fell on his knees before the spring, dipping up the water in his hands.

"What did you give him, professor?" grinned Tad.

"Hot drops!" answered the man of science tersely.

"Not that stuff you fed me when I ate too much honey in the Rockies?" questioned Stacy.

"The same."

"Wow! I had ten drops and it felt like a pailful when it got inside of me."

"How much did you give Juan?" questioned Walter.

"Twenty drops," answered Professor Zepplin without the suspicion of a smile on his face this time.

The Pony Rider Boys added their yells to those of the guide, only with a difference. The more Juan drank of the spring water, the more did the hot drops burn.

All at once he sprang up and started for the plain.

"Catch him!" commanded the Professor.

With a shout the lads started in pursuit. They overhauled the guide some twenty rods from camp, he having proved himself fleet of foot. Then again, the fire within him perhaps helped to increase his natural speed.

"I burn! I burn!" he wailed as the boys grabbed and laughingly hustled him back to camp.

"You'll burn worse than that if you ever ask for liquor in this outfit," retorted Ned. "We don't use the stuff, nor do we allow anyone around us who does."

"How do you feel now?" grinned the Professor as they came up to him with their prisoner.

"He's got a whole camp-fire in his little estomago," announced Chunky solemnly, which sally elicited a loud laugh from the boys.

"Give him some olive oil," directed the Professor. "I think the lesson has been sufficiently burned into him."

But considerable persuasion was necessary to induce Juan to take a spoonful of the Professor's medicine. He had already had one sample of it and he did not want another. Yet after some urging he tasted of the oil, at first gingerly; then he took it down at a gulp.

"Ah!" he breathed.

"Is it good?" grinned Tad.

"Si. Much burn, much burn," he explained, rubbing his stomach.

"Think you want some liquor still, Juan, or would you prefer another dose of my magic drops?"

"No, no, no, señor!" cried Juan, hastily moving away from Professor Zepplin.

"Very well; any time when you feel a longing for strong drink, just help yourself to the hot drops," said the Professor, striding away to his tent, medicine case in hand.

The guide, a much chastened man, set about assisting in getting the evening meal, but the hot drops still remained with him, making their presence known by occasional hot twinges.

Supper that night was an enjoyable affair, though it was observed that the guide did not eat heartily.

"Do you think he really had a pain?" asked Walter confidentially, leaning toward Ned.

"Pain? No. He wanted something else."

"And he got it," added Stacy, nodding solemnly.

A chorus of "he dids" ran around the table, stopping only when they reached Juan himself.

CHAPTER III.
INDIANS!

"Juan, did you see two men get off the train at Bluewater yesterday when we did? One of them had a big, broad sombrero like mine?" asked Tad, riding up beside the guide next day while they were crossing the range.

"Si."

"Know them?"

"Si," he replied, holding up one finger.

"You mean you know one of them?"

The guide nodded.

"Who is he?"

"Señor Lasar."

"Lasar. What's his other name?"

"Juan not know."

"Did they stop in the village?"

"No. Señors get ponies, ride over mountain," and the guide pointed lazily to the south-west.

"Where did they go? Do you know?"

Juan shrugged his shoulders, indicating that he did not.

"What is Mr. Lasar's business?"

Again the guide answered with a shrug. He seemed disinclined to discuss the man in whom Tad Butler was so much interested. Up to that time the lad had been too fully occupied with other matters to think of the conversation he and Stacy had overheard on the Atlantic and Pacific train. Now it came back to him with full force.

"Know anybody by the name of Marquand in this country?" he asked, taking another tack.

Juan said he did not, and then Tad gave up his questioning.

"I was asking Juan about the two men who sat ahead of us in the train yesterday," he explained to Chunky, as the fat boy joined them.

"Wha'd he say?"

"One is named Lasar, but he did not know the other one. I can't help believing that those fellows were plotting to do some one a great injury."

"So do I," agreed Chunky. "I guess we had better not say anything about it to the others, but we'll try to find out who this man Lasar is, and who Mr. Marquand is. Then we'll decide what to do next."

Their further conversation was interrupted by the voice of the Professor, announcing that they would halt for their noonday meal. All other thoughts left the mind of Stacy Brown when the question of food was raised. He quickly slipped from his pony, running back to hurry the burros along so as to hasten the meal for which he was yearning. Only one burro was unpacked, as it was the intention of the outfit to push on soon after finishing their lunch.

While the guide, under Ned's direction, was making it ready, Tad and Chunky strolled off to climb a high rock that they had seen in the vicinity and which, they thought, might give them a good view of the plains to the southwest on the other side of the range.

They had promised to be back in half an hour, but circumstances arose that caused them to delay their return considerably.

After threshing through the bushes, over sharp rocks and through miniature canyons, they gained at last the object of their quest. The distance had been further than they had imagined.

"We'll have to make a short trip of it up to the top and back," said Tad. "It has taken us almost all our time to get here. But we'll have a look, anyway."

They soon gained the top of the rock, which stood some twenty feet higher than the crest of the mountain on which it rested.

"Isn't this great?" exclaimed Tad.

"Might think we were in the Rockies."

"Or the Ozarks."

"I hope we don't have as much trouble here as we did in that range. Our guide is not much better than the Shawnee we had for a time on that trip. I can't see the foothills, but the plain on beyond is pretty clear."

"Hope we don't have to chase all over the desert for water. I—"

Tad grasped his companion by the sleeve and jerked him violently to the rock.

"What's up? What's the matter with you?" protested Stacy.

"Keep still, some one's coming."

The lad's keen ears had caught a sound which Stacy had entirely failed to hear. It was the sound of horses making their way through the bushes. There were several in the party, Tad could tell by the sounds, and having in mind the man Lasar, he thought he might perhaps learn something of advantage by remaining quietly on the top of the rock.

All this he explained in a few brief words to his companion. Then both boys crouched low, peering over the cliff, having first removed their sombreros.

What they saw, a few moments later, surprised them very much indeed.

The horsemen in single file suddenly appeared out of a draw to the east and headed for the rock where the lads were in hiding.

"Look! Look!" exclaimed Tad in a low, suppressed voice.

"I-n-d-i-a-n-s!" breathed Chunky.

They seemed to rise right up out of the ground, as one by one they emerged from the draw to the more level rocks that lay about the hiding place of the Pony Rider Boys.

"I wonder who they are?" questioned Tad.

"They look savage. I wonder if they'd hurt us, Tad?"

"I don't know. I do know, though, that I wouldn't trust those ugly faces one second. I thought the Blackfeet were savage, but they're not to be compared with these redskins."

A full dozen of them had, by this time, come into view. They sat huddled on their ponies, their painted faces just appearing above the gayly colored blankets in which they were enveloped.

"They must be cold," muttered Chunky. "Shouldn't think they'd need bed clothes around them this time of the year."

"Not so loud, Chunky," warned Tad.

"Know what they are, Tad?"

"I wouldn't say positively, but somehow they look to me like Apaches."

Tad's surmise was correct. The twelve warriors were members of the savage band that had in past years caused the Government so much trouble and bloodshed.

"They're off their reservation, if they are Apaches," whispered the lad.

"What does that indicate, Tad?"

"I don't know. They may be on the warpath; then, again, they may be down here after game. I'm not sure even, if there is any game here. We'll lie still until they get by us. That's the best plan; don't you think so?"

"Yes."

"Lie perfectly still, Chunky. The little bushes in front of us will screen us, providing we don't move about. Indians have quick eyes, though they do look as if they were half asleep."

"They're getting off their horses, Tad. What does that mean?"

"I don't know."

Tad peered through the bushes, noting every move that the redskins made. At first he thought they had discovered him and were about to surround the rock and take him prisoner. But he soon saw that such was not their intention. Tethering their ponies, the Indians cast their blankets on the ground, after having first picked out a suitable place.

"They're making camp," whispered Tad.

One after another of the savages took out his pipe, and soon the odor from burning tobacco was wafted to the nostrils of the hidden Pony Rider Boys.

"Guess they're going to get some dinner," decided Stacy, observing that the strangers were gathering brush.

This was the case. The ponies had been staked where they could browse on the green leaves, and now their masters were about to satisfy their own appetites.

Tad groaned.

"What is it?" questioned Stacy apprehensively.

"They will be here half of the day at least. I know a little about Indians, having been captured by them once. The difference is that my Indians were in a hurry to get somewhere. These fellows seem to have all the time in the world. They're waiting—killing time for some reason. You'll see, after they finish their dinner, that they will smoke some more, then lie down for a catnap."

"And—and what'll we be doing?"

"We'll be hiding on the top of this rock, Chunky."

"Wish I had my rifle."

"Lucky for both of us that you haven't."

The lads had been talking in whispers, but the words fairly froze in their mouths, when, upon glancing down they saw the eyes of a savage fixed upon them.

"On your life, don't move a muscle, Chunky," whispered Tad, as soon as he had recovered his wits.

Tad was not sure that the Indian saw them, yet there could be no doubt that the savage eyes were burning into their very own.

Soon, however, the Indian dropped his glances to his pipe bowl and the boys breathed a sigh of relief.

"Don't move yet, Chunky," directed Tad.

It was a wise command, for almost instantly the Indian glanced in their direction again, and, as if satisfied, emptied his pipe and stretched out on his blanket. The two lads breathed sighs of relief.

"Did he see us, do you think, Tad?"

"No. At first he thought he saw something up here, but he changed his mind after a little, as you observed."

By this time the redskins were cooking their midday meal, and the odor nearly drove Stacy frantic. It made him realize how hungry he was. He pulled a leaf from a bush and began chewing it in hopes of wearing off the keen edge of his appetite.

"How long we got to stay here?" he demanded. "I've a good notion to get up and walk back to camp. They don't dare hurt us."

"Lie still!" commanded his companion sternly. "I have a plan that we may be able to put into operation. We can't do it now, though."

The lads waited, Tad almost with the patience of an Indian, Chunky ill at ease and restless.

"Can't you lie still? What ails you?"

"My stomach's fighting my appetite. Hear 'em growl at each other?"

"S-h-h-h."

"I don't care. I'd 'bout as soon be scalped as to starve to death."

The braves had by now filled their stomachs, gulping their food down without the formality of chewing it at all. Stacy's amazement was partly mixed with admiration as he observed the food disappear with such rapidity.

Now the braves had begun puffing at their pipes. After a time, one by one laid down his smoking bowl and stretched himself out for a nap, just as Tad had said they would. The savages were spread out so that they had a very good view of three sides of the rock on which the two lads were perched, but the fourth side was hidden from them. Tad decided that, as the Indians showed no intention of moving, they were going to remain where they were until night.

"I want you to follow me, Chunky," Butler said, determined to try his plan. "You will have to move absolutely without a sound. Look before you put down foot or hand. Be sure where you place them. We'll wait a few minutes until they're sound asleep."

"What you going to do—sneak?"

"Try to get back to camp. The others will be coming along looking for us pretty soon, if we don't get away. The Indians might resent being disturbed, and perhaps make trouble."

"Tell me when you're ready, then."

Some minutes had elapsed and the lads could plainly hear the snores of their besiegers.

"Now!" whispered Tad.

At the same time he began crawling toward the edge of the rock at their rear. Stacy was close upon his heels.

The side which the boys were to descend was much more precipitous than the one they had come up by, but offered no very great difficulties for two nimble boys. Proceeding with infinite caution, they gained the ground without a mishap.

"We'll walk straight on in this direction, until we get out of sight; then we can turn to the left and hurry to the camp."

Stacy nodded. As he did so his eyes were off the ground for a few seconds. Those few seconds proved his undoing.

The lad stepped on a stone that gave way under him, turning his ankle almost upon its side.

"Ouch!" yelled Chunky.

"Now you've done it," snapped Tad. "We'll have the whole pack of them down on us. Can you walk?"

"I—I don't know. I'll try."

"Take hold of my hand. You've got to run."

The redskins were on their feet in an instant. A few bounds carried them around the rock whence the exclamation had come. By this time Tad had dragged his companion into the bushes but not quickly enough to elude the keen eyes of the savages.

The Indians uttered a short, sharp cry, then aimed their rifles at the figures of the two fleeing Pony Rider Boys.

Tad saw the movement. He threw himself prone upon the ground, jerking Chunky down beside him.

They were screened from the eyes of the enemy, for the moment.

"Crawl! Crawl!" commanded Tad.

On hands and feet the boys began running rapidly over the ground, on down into a narrow gulch. If they could gain the opposite side they would be safe, as it was unlikely that the Indians would follow them there. To do so, the boys were obliged to cross an open space. They had just reached it, when their pursuers appeared behind them. Once more the Indians raised their rifles, their fingers exerting a gentle pressure on the triggers.

CHAPTER IV.
ON THE TRAIL OF JUAN

"Look out! They're going to shoot!" cried Tad.

The lads quickly rolled in opposite directions.

"Hallo-o, Tad!"

The call was in the stentorian voice of Professor Zepplin, to which Ned Rector added a shout of his own.

Fearing that some ill had befallen Tad and Stacy, the others had started out after them. Following them came Walter and the lazy Mexican.

"We're down here! Look out for the Indians!" warned Tad in a loud voice.

"You're crazy!" jeered Ned. "Come out of that. What ails you fellows? The dinner's stone cold and Professor Zepplin is all in the stew."

Tad scrambled to his feet, with a quick glance at the top of the ridge, where, but a moment before, half a dozen rifles had been leveled at Chunky and himself.

Not an Indian was in sight. Tad was amazed. He could not understand it. Grabbing Stacy by an arm he hurried him up the other side of the gulch, where they quickly joined their companions.

"What does this mean?" demanded the Professor.

"Hurry! We must get out of this. It's Indians!"

"They—they wanted to scalp us," interjected Stacy.

"But you runned away, eh? Brave man!" chuckled Ned.

"Indians! There are no Indians here."

"I'll tell you about it when we get to camp. They were just about to shoot at us when you appeared up here."

"'Pache bad Injun," vouchsafed Juan.

"Were those Apaches?" questioned Tad.

The guide shrugged his shoulders.

"I was sure they were, though I do not think I ever saw an Apache before. They don't live about here, do they, Juan?"

"'Pache off reservation. Him go dance. Firewater! Ugh!" making a motion as if scalping himself.

"I'm hungry," called Stacy.

"Yes; so am I," added Tad. "But I think we had better not wait to eat. We can take a bite in the saddle while we are moving."

Stacy protested loudly at this, but Tad's judgment prevailed with the Professor, after the boys had related their experience in detail. All hands began at once to pack up the few belongings that had been taken from the burro, and once more they started on their way, moving somewhat more rapidly than had been the case in the early part of the day.

"I don't suppose there will be much use in our hurrying, Professor," said the lad, after they had been going a short time. "I know enough about Indians to be sure those fellows will follow us until they satisfy themselves who and what we are. They are up to some mischief, and they thought we were spying on them. Otherwise, I do not believe they would have tried to shoot us. Don't know as you could blame them much."

"I am inclined to agree with you, Master Tad. It will be good policy not to pay any attention to them if we discover any of them. Just go right along about our business as if we didn't see them at all."

"And you're not likely to," grinned Tad. "Where did you say they were going, Juan?"

"'Pache, go dance."

"He means they're bound for a pow-wow somewhere. That explains it," nodded the lad.

The rest of the day passed without incident. Not a sign of the Indians did the boys see. As a matter of fact, the roving redskins were as anxious to keep out of the sight of the Pony Riders as the boys were to have them do so.

The party enjoyed the trip over the mountains immensely; and, when, a few days later, they made camp in the foothills on the southern side of the Zuni range, the boys declared that they had never had a better time.

Professor Zepplin decided that they would remain in that camp for a couple of days, as he desired to make some scientific investigations and collect geological specimens. This suited the rest of the party, who were free to make as many side trips as they wished, into mountain fastnesses or over the plains to the south of them.

Early in the day the guide asked permission to go away for an hour or so. They noticed that he had been uneasy, apparently anxious to get away for some reason unknown to them.

"He's got something up his sleeve," decided Tad, eyeing Juan narrowly.

"You may go, but we shall expect you back in time for the noon meal," the Professor told him.

"Give me money," requested the guide.

"Certainly. Let me see, you have worked a week. I gave you five dollars when we started out. You were to have ten dollars a week while you were with us. That leaves five dollars due you," announced the Professor.

"Me work week. Me want ten dollars."

"But, my man, I've already paid you five dollars, which pays you for half of the week. Here is the five dollars for the other half. That's all I owe you. Do you understand?"

"Si señor. But Juan work one week," protested the guide.

"Let me show him," interrupted Tad. He drew ten marks in the sand with a stick, separating them into two groups of five. "Here are ten marks, Juan. We'll call them ten dollars. Understand?"

"Si."

"Well, here are the first five marks in the dirt that the Professor paid you. How many does that leave?"

"Five," gleamed the white teeth.

"Right. Go to the head of the class," interrupted Stacy.

"Chunky, you keep out of this. You'll mix him up."

"Guess somebody's mixed up already," retorted the fat boy.

"Five is right," continued Tad. "Five dollars is what we owe you. Is that clear now?"

"Si, señor. But I work one week. Juan earn ten dollar—"

"I'll tell you what to do," interjected Ned. "Start all over again. You begin work to-day; Juan, and we'll pay you ten dollars for every week from now on. You haven't worked for us before to-day, you know."

The lads laughed heartily, but Juan merely showed his teeth, protesting that he had earned ten dollars.

"Here," said Tad, thrusting a five dollar bill at him. "You take this. It's all we owe you. If you see any of your friends, you ask them how much we owe you. They'll tell you the Professor is right."

Juan took the money greedily, still protesting that they owed him ten dollars, because he had worked a week. Mounting his burro, he rode away; at once falling into the marvelous speed that he had shown them on the first day out.

The lads shouted with laughter as they saw burro and rider disappear among the foothills, both running for all they were worth, Juan uttering his shrill "yi-yi's," as he pedaled the ground.

That was the last they saw of the Mexican guide that day. The rest of the day was employed in games, trick riding, rope throwing and the like. Stacy found some horned frogs, which were of considerable interest to the boys. Chunky made the discovery that the frogs liked to have their backs scratched with a stick, and the frogs of the foothills probably never spent such a happy day in all their lives as Chunky and his stick provided for them that afternoon.

Late in the day, it dawned upon the boys that Juan was still absent. They consulted with the Professor about this, upon his return from a collecting trip along the foot of the mountains. But the Professor was sure Juan would be in in time for supper.

Such was not the case, however. After the meal had been finished Tad announced his intention of riding off in the direction Juan had gone, to see if the guide could not be found.

"I'll go with you," announced Stacy.

"All right; come along," said Tad, tightening his saddle girths. "We'll have a fine gallop."

"Be careful that you do not get lost, boys," warned the Professor.

"Can't get lost. All we have to do is to follow the foothills. We shall probably find Juan and his burro sound asleep on an ant-hill somewhere. He's positively the laziest human being I ever set eyes on."

"Better take along five dollars to bait him with," suggested Ned.

"I've got my stick," said Stacy. "I'll tickle the back of the burro and its rider, just as I did the frogs."

"You try that on the burro and he'll kick you into the middle of next week," warned Walter.

"Yes," laughed Tad. "Did you see him kick when Juan tossed a tomato can against his heels this morning? Kicked the can clear over a tree and out of sight."

"He'd make a good batter for the Chillicothe baseball team," suggested Chunky. "He'd be the only real batter in the nine. They could turn him loose on the umpire when they didn't need him on the diamond. Wouldn't it be funny to see some umpires kicked over the high board fence?"

"Come along if you are going with me."

Stacy swung into his saddle, and, galloping off, caught up with Tad, who was in a hurry to get back to camp before dark.

"Keep your eyes to the right, Chunky, and I'll look on the left. If you see anything that looks like a lazy Mexican and a lazy burro, just call out."

"I'll run over them, that's what I'll do," declared the fat boy. "Hello, there's a fellow on horseback."

"I see him."

The lads changed their course a little so as to head off the solitary horseman, who was loping along in something of a hurry.

"Howdy," greeted the lad.

"Evening, stranger. Where you hail from and where to?"

"We're in camp back here. I'm looking for our guide, a Mexican named Juan. He went away this morning and we haven't seen him since."

"And you won't so long as his money holds out," laughed the horseman.

"Then, you've seen him? Will you tell me where I may find him?"

"Sure thing, boy, but I reckon you'd better not be going any further?"

"Why not?"

"He's over yonder, gambling with some renegade Apaches."

"Apaches!" exclaimed the lads in one voice. "Those must be the same fellows we saw up in the range. But how do you suppose he knew they were over there?"

"He? Those Greasers know everything except what they ought to know—especially if there's any games of chance going on."

"Will you please tell me how we can reach the place? We want to make a very early start in the morning, and I don't like to take a chance of his not getting back in time."

"If ye're bound to go, keep right along the edge of the foothills. You can't miss the place. Better keep away if you don't want to be getting into a mix-up. There's going to be lively doings over there pretty soon," warned the stranger.

"How do you mean? I've seen Indians before. Guess they won't hurt us if they let Juan pow-wow with them."

"This is different, young man. They're going to hold a fire dance to-night—"

"A fire dance?"

"Yes."

"I thought they weren't allowed to do that any more?"

"They ain't, but they will. There's a bunch of Sabobas from over the line. They're the original fire eaters. They come over here kind of secret like. Then there's Pueblos, 'Paches, and bad ones from every tribe within a hundred miles of here. Been making smoke signals from the mountains for more'n a week past—"

"I saw that yesterday and thought it was intended as a signal."

"Right."

"But you don't think there will be any danger in just going after our guide, do you?"

"Boy, they'll be letting blood before morning, even if the Government doesn't drop down on the picnic and clean out the whole bunch of them. There is sure to be trouble before morning."

"Thank you," said Tad, touching his pony;

"Going on?" questioned the horseman.

"Yes; I'm going to fetch Juan," replied Tad, touching spurs to his pony and galloping away, followed by Stacy Brown.

The horseman sat his saddle watching the receding forms of the two Pony Rider Boys until they disappeared behind a butte in the foothills.

"Well, if those kids ain't got the sand!" he muttered.

CHAPTER V.
A DARING ACT

"If you don't want to go with me you may go back, Chunky. Perhaps one would not be as likely to get into trouble as two. You can find your way, can't you?"

"I go back? Think I'm a tenderfoot? Huh! Guess I ain't afraid of any cheap Wild West Indians. I'm going with you, Tad."

"Very well; but see to it that you keep in the background. You have a habit of getting into trouble on the slightest provocation."

"So do you," retorted Stacy.

The ponies had been urged to their best pace by this time. Twilight had fallen and darkness would settle over them in a very short time now, though a new moon hovered pale and weak in the blue sky above. Tad knew this, so he did not worry about the return trip.

"We should be sighting the place pretty soon," he muttered.

"I see a light," announced Stacy.

"Where?"

"To the right. Over that low butte there."

"Yes; that's so. I see it now. You have sharp eyes," laughed Tad.

"I can see when there's anything to see."

"And eat when there's food to be had," added Tad.

"Think those are the Indians that wanted to shoot us, Tad?" he asked, with a trace of apprehension in his voice.

Tad glanced at his companion keenly;

"Getting cold feet, Chunky?"

"No!" roared the fat boy.

"I beg your pardon," grinned Tad. "I didn't mean to insult you."

"Better not. Look out that you don't get chilblains on your own feet. May need a hot mustard bath yourself before you get through."

They rounded the butte. A full quarter of a mile ahead of them flickered a large fire, with several smaller blazes twinkling here and there about it. Shadowy figures were observed moving back and forth, some with rapid movements, others in slow, methodical steps.

"There must be a lot of them, Tad."

"Looks that way. I wonder where we shall find the guide."

Both boys fell silent for a time, and as they drew nearer to the scene pulled their ponies down to a walk. Tad concluded to make a detour half way round the camp in order to get a clump of bushes that he had observed between them and the redskins. From that point of vantage he would be able to get a closer view, and perhaps locate the man for whom he was looking.

Riding in, they were soon swallowed up in the shadows.

"Hold my pony a moment," directed Tad, slipping to the ground.

"Where are you going?"

"Nowhere, just this minute. I'm going to look around."

The lad peered through the bushes until, uttering a low exclamation, he turned to his companion.

"I see him. He's over on the other side—"

"Who? Juan?"

"Yes. Now I want you to remain right here. Don't move away. I'll tie my pony so he won't give you any trouble. Sit perfectly quiet, and if any Indians come along don't bother them. I'm going around the outside, so I don't have to pass through the crowd, though they seem too busy to notice anyone."

Tad slipped away in the shadows until he came to a spot opposite where he had caught a glimpse of the lazy Mexican.

He discovered Juan in the center of a circle of dusky Indians who were squatting on the ground. Some of the braves were clothed in nondescript garments, while others were attired in gaudy blankets. These were the gamblers.

At that moment their efforts were concentrated on winning from Juan the wages of his first week's work with the Pony Rider Boys. A blanket had been spread over the ground, and on this they were wagering small amounts on the throw of the dice, a flickering campfire near by dimly lighting up the blanket and making the reading of the dice a difficult matter for any but the keenest of eyes. The singsong calls of the players added to the weirdness of the scene.

Tad waited long enough to observe that the guide lost nearly every time, the stolid-faced red men raking in his coins with painful regularity.

"It's a wonder he has a cent left. But they're not playing for very large amounts, as near as I can tell."

Each time the Mexican lost he would utter a shrill "si, si," then lured by the hope that Dame Fortune would favor him, reached greedily for the next throw.

"It's time for me to do something," muttered Tad.

Stepping boldly from his cover, he walked up to the edge of the circle.

"Juan!" he called sharply.

"Si," answered the Mexican, without looking up.

"Juan!"

This time the word was uttered in a more commanding voice.

"You come with me!"

The guide, oblivious to all beyond the terrible fascination of the game he was playing, gave no heed to Tad Butler's stern command. Three times did Tad call to him, but without result. One of the red men cast an angry glance in the Tad's direction, and then returned to his play.

Without an instant's hesitation, Tad sprang over into the center of the circle, and grasping Juan by an ear, jerked him to his feet.

Red hands fell to belts and dark faces scowled menacingly at the intruder.

"You come with me, Juan!"

Juan sought to jerk away, but under the strong pull on his ear, he did not find it advisable to force himself from his captor's grip.

"You ought to be ashamed of yourself. You're lucky if Professor Zepplin doesn't give you another dose of hot drops for this. I suppose these Indians sat down to rob you," growled Tad.

"No, no, no," protested Juan.

By this time the Indian gamblers had leaped to their feet, an ugly light in their eyes that boded ill for the Pony Rider Boy who had interrupted them in the process of fleecing the Mexican.

With one accord they barred the way in a solid human wall. Tad found himself hemmed in on all sides. It had been easy to gain an entrance to the circle, but getting out of it was another matter.

"This man belongs to me," he said with as much courage in his tone as he was able to command. "You will please step aside and let us go. You're breaking the law. If you offer any resistance I'll have the government officers after you in short order."

He could not have said a worse thing under the circumstances. At first they took him for a spy, possibly a Government spy. Now they were sure of it, for had not the lad told them so himself?

With a growl, one who appeared to be the most important personage in the group drew his sheath knife and sprang straight at the slender figure of Tad Butler.

Tad acted without an instant's hesitation.

Stepping aside quickly; he cleverly avoided the knife-thrust. At the same instant, while the Indian was off his balance, not yet having recovered from the lunge, the Pony Rider Boy's fist and the Indian's jaw met in sudden collision.

The impact of the blow might have been heard more than a rod away.

The red man's blanket dropped from his shoulders; he staggered backward, made a supreme effort to pull himself together, then dropped in a heap at the feet of the boy who had felled him.

Without waiting for the astonished red gamblers to recover their wits, Tad grasped an arm of the Mexican and sprang away into the bushes.

He had done a serious thing, even though in self-protection. He had knocked down an Apache brave with his fist. The sting of that blow would rest upon the savage jaw until the insult was wiped out by the victim himself.

CHAPTER VI.
THE FIRE DANCE OF THE RED MEN

The Indians made a sudden move to pursue the lad who had done so daring a thing. One of their number restrained them, pointing to the fallen brave, as much as to say, "Revenge is for *him!*"

With a shrug of their shoulders the Indians sank down and resumed their game as stoically as before. They gave no further heed to the unconscious Apache, who still lay just outside the circle where he had been knocked out by Tad's blow.

"Hurry! Hurry!" commanded the lad, fairly dragging his companion along. "They'll be after us in a minute."

Yet before the minute had elapsed Tad had halted suddenly, his wondering eyes fixed upon the scene that was being enacted before him.

About a pit of red hot coals, naked save for the breech clouts they wore, swayed the bodies of half-a-dozen powerful braves.

They were the fire dancers and Tad was gazing upon a scene that probably never will be seen again in this country—the last of the fire dances—a secret dance of which it was to be supposed the Government agents knew nothing.

Back and forth waved the copper-colored line, right up to the edge of the pit of glowing coals, uttering a weird chant, which was taken up by others who were not in the dance.

The voices of the chanters grew louder, their excitement waxed higher, as the thrill of song and dance pulsed through their veins.

All at once, Tad was horrified to see one of the dancers leap into the air, uttering a mighty shriek. While still clear of the ground the dancer's body turned, then he dove head first into the bed of hot coals. He was out in an instant.

The chant rose higher as the remaining dancers followed the leader into the burning pit and out of it. So quickly did they move that they seemed not to feel the heat, and from Tad's point of vantage, he was sure that none was burned in the slightest.

Juan tried to pull away. But Tad held him in a firm grip.

Now that the dancers had passed through the fire unscathed, others followed them, some no more than touching the live coals, then bounding out on the other side of the pit; others remaining long enough to roll swiftly across the glowing bed.

Excitement was rapidly waxing higher and higher. The red men were in a dangerous mood. It boded ill for the paleface who sought to interfere with their carnival at this moment.

"Come!" whispered Tad in a low, tense voice. "We've got to get out of this mighty quick! Chunky's probably half scared to death, too."

Tad did not go far. He had scarcely taken half a dozen steps when a frenzied yell, a series of shrill shrieks sounded in the air. The sounds seemed to come from all directions at once.

"What's that?"

"Me not know."

"Somebody's running a pony. I hear it coming. It's headed right for that bunch of crazy savages. Probably an Indian gone mad."

It was not an Indian who was the cause of this new disturbance, as the lad discovered almost immediately afterward.

"Yip, yip! Y-e-o-w! W-o-w!"

The yells were uttered in the shrill voice of Stacy Brown.

"It's Chunky!" groaned Tad. "Here's trouble in earnest!"

They never knew just how it happened, and Chunky could not tell them, but in all probability the excitement had been too much for the fat boy!

He had moved closer when the dancing began, and the fever of it got into his veins until his excitement had reached a pitch beyond his control.

With a series of howls and yells, the fat boy drove the rowels of the spurs deep into his pony's aides.

The animal dashed forward at a break-neck pace.

Stacy headed straight for the glowing pit, yelling with every leap of the pony.

Tad gazed spellbound. He seemed powerless to move. He had been deeply affected by the scenes he had seen; but this was different. The lad held his breath.

Reaching the edge of the pit, Stacy's pony rose in the air, clearing the bed of coals in a long, curving leap.

Two red men had just risen from their fiery bath. The hind hoofs of the pony caught and bowled them over.

"Run to the camp and get help! Take my pony! Ride for your life! Don't lose a second!" gasped Tad, giving the lazy Mexican a shove that sent him stumbling until he had measured his length upon the ground.

Juan picked himself up slowly; and, crawling away into the bushes, lay down to rest or hide.

Stacy's pony landed fairly in the center of a bunch of half-clothed savages; some of whom went down under the pony when it landed on them so unexpectedly.

The next instant the fat boy had been jerked from the animal's back, to which he was clinging desperately.

With a yell the redskins hurled him toward the fire. But the force of the throw had not been quite strong enough. Stacy landed on the edge of the pit, rolling half into it, the upper part of his body being on the ground to which he was hanging, yelling lustily. His shod feet were in the fire, however, but as yet he did not realize that his clothes were burning.

Tad Butler sprang quickly from his hiding place.

"Crawl out!" he roared. "You'll be burned alive!"

"I—I can't. I fell in," piped Stacy, all his bravery gone now.

Tad leaped across the intervening space and bounded to the side of his companion.

"Ouch! I'm on fire!" shrieked Stacy.

Tad grabbed and hauled him from his dangerous position. One of Tad's feet slipped in while he was doing so. By this time the clothes of both lads had begun to smoulder.

"Run for it! Better be burned than scalped!" shouted Tad.

Holding to Chunky's arm the Pony Rider Boy started to run. He was tripped by a moccasined foot before they had gone ten feet. Both boys fell headlong. Ere they could rise half a dozen mad savages were upon them.

The lads were jerked roughly to their feet, Chunky shivering, Tad pale but resolute. There was nothing that he could say or do to repair the damage that his companion had done.

One whom the lad took to be a chief, from his head-dress and commanding appearance, pushed his way into the crowd about the two boys, hurling the red men aside with reckless sweeps of his powerful arms.

"Ugh!" he grunted, folding his arms and gazing sternly at the two prisoners.

"Who you?"

Tad explained as best he could.

"Why you do this?"

"My friend here got excited," Tad declared.

"Huh! Lie!"

Tad's face burned. He could scarcely resist the impulse to resent the imputation that the savage had cast upon him. He conquered the inclination with an effort.

"Sir, we had no wish to interfere with you. We came here to get one of our men who had come here to gamble. If you will release us we will return to our camp and give you no further trouble. I promise you that."

"T-h-h-h-at's so," chattered Chunky.

"Keep still," whispered Tad. "You'll get us into more trouble."

The chief appeared to be debating the question in his own mind, when one of the men, whom Tad recognized as a member of the gambling circle, whispered something to the chief.

The chief's eyes blazed. Uttering a succession of gutteral sounds, he gave some quick directions to the red men near him.

"He makes a noise like a litter of pigs," muttered Chunky.

Acting upon the chief's direction two braves grabbed the lads, and hurried them away, Tad meanwhile watching for an opportunity to break away. Had he been alone, he felt sure he could do so safely. But he would not leave his companion, of course.

The Apaches took the boys a short distance from the camp, planked them down roughly with their backs to a rock.

"Now, I wonder what next?" muttered Tad.

While one of the braves stood guard over them, the second trotted back to the camp, returning after a few minutes with a third savage who carried a rifle.

The boys were sure then that they were to be shot.

"Huh! You run, brave shoot um!" warned one of the first pair, after which parting injunction the two captors strode away, leaving their companion to guard the boys.

For a few moments the Indian walked up and down in front of them, keeping his eyes fixed on the lads. Tad noted that he walked rather unsteadily. Finally, the guard sat down facing them, some ten feet away.

"Well, you've certainly gone and done it this time, Chunky," said Tad in a low voice. "What on earth made you do a crazy thing like that?"

"I—I don't know."

"Well, it's too late for regrets. All we can do will be to make the best of our situation and watch for an opportunity to get away."

For several minutes the boys sat gazing at the stolid figure before them. Tad's mind was working, though his body was not.

"Make believe you're going to sleep, but don't overdo it," whispered Tad.

This was something that Stacy could do, and he did it with such naturalness that Tad could not repress a smile.

"That Indian is dazed from his excitement, and if we make him think we're asleep he's likely to relax his vigilance," mused Tad, as the two boys gradually leaned closer together, soon to all appearances being wrapped in sleep. Little by little the Indian's head nodded.

Finally he toppled over to one side, the rifle lying across his feet.

Tad and Chunky remained motionless.

The Indian snored.

The boys waited. Soon the snores became regular. The moment for action had arrived.

Tad pinched Chunky.

"Huh! Wat'cher want?"

The fat boy had in reality been asleep.

"For goodness sake, keep quiet!" begged Tad in a whisper. "Don't you know there's an Indian with a gun guarding us? He's asleep. Come, but be quiet if you value your life at all. Anyway; remember that I want to save mine."

Stacy was wide awake now. Together the lads crawled cautiously away, every nerve on the alert. Over by the pit of live coals the uproar was, if any thing, louder than before.

The boys gave that part of the camp a wide berth.

"Now get up and run!" commanded Tad. "Raise your feet off the ground, so that you won't fall over every pebble you come to."

Tad and Chunky clasped hands and scurried through the bushes, making as little noise as possible, and rapidly putting considerable distance between them and the sleeping red man who had been set to watch them.

"Having lots of fun, ain't we, Tad?"

"Fun! You're lucky if you get off with a whole scalp—"

"Wow!" exclaimed Stacy.

The lads brought up suddenly.

At first they were not sure what had disturbed them, that is, Tad was not. This time Stacy had seen more clearly than his companion.

"Ugh!" grunted a voice right in front of them, and there before their amazed eyes stood an Indian. To their imaginations, he was magnified until he appeared nearly as tall as the moonlit mountains in the background.

For one hesitating instant the lads stood staring at the figure looming over them.

With an angry growl the red man bounded toward them. He had recognized the boys and was determined that they should not escape him.

It was Stacy Brown's wits that saved the situation this time. As the Indian came at them the fat boy dived between the savage's naked legs, uttering a short, sharp yelp, for all the world just like that of a small dog attempting to frighten off a bigger antagonist.

There could be only one result following Chunky's unexpected tactics. Mr. Redskin flattened himself on the ground prone upon his face. Somehow the fellow was slightly stunned by the fall, not having had time to save himself from a violent bump on the head.

"Run for it, Chunky! He'll be after us in a second."

The lads made a lively sprint for the open. In a moment, observing that they were not being followed, they halted, still in the shadows of the bushes. All at once Tad stumbled over an object in the dark. At first he thought it was another Indian, and both boys were about to run again, when the voice of the prostrate man caused them to laugh instead.

"Si, si, señor," muttered the fellow.

"Juan? It's Juan! Get up! You here yet?"

They pulled the lazy guide to his feet, starting off with him, when all at once Tad happened to think that one of the ponies was back there somewhere among the Indians.

"You stay here, and don't make a fool of yourself this time!" commanded Tad.

"Where are you going?"

"After your pony. You hang on to Juan. I'll hold you responsible for him, Chunky."

"Guess I can take care of a lazy Mexican if I can floor a redskin," answered Stacy proudly.

But Tad was off. He had not heard the last remark of his companion. In picking his way carefully around the camp to where he had seen a lot of ponies tethered, Tad found a Navajo blanket. He quickly possessed himself of it, throwing it over his head, wrapping himself in its folds.

He was now in plain sight of the wild antics of the dancers, who, still mad with the excitement of the hour, were performing all manner of weird movements. For a moment, the lad squatted down to watch them. He had been there but a short time when a voice at his side startled him, and Tad was about to take a fresh sprint when he realized that it was not the voice of a savage.

"Young man, you'd better light out of here while you've got the chance," said the stranger.

Turning sharply, Tad discovered a man, who, like himself, was wrapped in a gaudy blanket. He was unable to see the man's face, which was hidden under the Navajo.

"Who are you?" demanded the lad sharply.

"I'm an Indian agent. I only got wind of this proposed fire dance late this afternoon. These men will all be punished unless they return to their reservations peaceably. If they do, they will be let go with a warning."

"Do they know you're here?"

"They? Not much," laughed the agent.

"But supposing they ask you a question?"

"I can talk all the different tribal languages represented here. You'd better go now. Where are you from?"

Tad explained briefly.

"Well, you have had a narrow escape tonight. If they catch you again they'll make short work of you."

"They won't catch me. Thank you and good-bye."

"Don't go that way. Strike straight back; then you will have an open course."

"I'm going after my companion's pony. I think I know where to find it," answered Tad, wrapping the blanket about himself and stealing across an open moonlit space without attracting attention.

The Indian agent watched him curiously for a moment; then he rose and followed quickly after Tad.

"That boy is either a fool—which I don't think—or else he doesn't know the meaning of the word 'fear.'"

Tad did not find Stacy's pony where he had expected. Indian ponies were tethered all about, singly and in groups, while here and there one was left to graze where it would.

"What sort of a looking pony is yours?" questioned the agent, coming up to him.

"A roan."

"Then I think I know where he is. He was not like the horses in this vicinity, which attracted my attention to him."

The agent led the way, in a roundabout course, to the south side of the camp, where they began looking over the animals. Occasionally a redskin would pass them, but no one gave either the slightest heed.

"Here he is," whispered Tad.

"Lead him off. Don't mount just yet."

Tad did as the agent had suggested. But all at once something happened. Tad's blanket had dropped from his shoulders, revealing him in his true colors. An Indian uttered a yell. Tad sprang into his saddle and put spurs to the pony. In a moment more than a dozen redskins had mounted and started yelling after him, believing he was stealing a pony.

Tad headed away to the south to give his companions a chance to get out of the way, and the savages came in full cry after him.

CHAPTER VII.
FLEEING FROM THE ENEMY

A shrill cry was wafted to the boy.

After a few moments Tad realized that they were no longer on his trail. He knew the cry had been a signal, warning them to halt. What he did not know, however, was that the Indian agent had been responsible for the signal; that he in all probability had saved the boy's life.

The lad, after satisfying himself that the Indians had abandoned the chase, at once circled about, coming back to the point where he had left Chunky and the Mexican. They were both there waiting for him.

"What was all that row?" demanded the fat boy. "We were having a little horse race, that's all," grinned Tad grimly; "Hurry along, now."

They reached their own camp in safety an hour later. The two boys had much to relate, and as the narration proceeded, Professor Zepplin shook his head disapprovingly.

"Young gentlemen, much as I have enjoyed this summer's outing, it's a wonder I haven't had nervous prostration long before this. It'll be a load off my mind if I get you all back in Chillicothe without anything serious happening to you."

"I think," suggested Tad, "that we had better strike camp at once and move on. The moon is shining brightly, and Juan ought to have no trouble in leading the way."

"Yes; that will be an excellent idea. You think they may give as further trouble?" questioned the Professor.

"They may before morning. They're getting more ugly every minute."

"Everything worth while seems to happen when I am not around," protested Ned.

"Good thing you weren't along," replied Stacy. "You'd been scared stiff. It was no place for tenderfeet."

"You—you call me a tenderfoot?" snapped Ned, starting for him.

"Stop quarreling, you two!" commanded Tad. "We've had all the fighting we want for one night. Get busy and help strike this camp. Guess none of this outfit could truthfully be called a tenderfoot. We've all had our share of hard knocks, and we'll have enough to look back to and think about when we get home and have time to go over our experiences together this winter."

The thought, that at any minute the half-crazed savages might sweep down on them hastened the preparations for departure. The Pony Rider Boys never struck camp more quickly than they did in the soft southern moonlight that night.

All at once Juan set up a wail.

"What is it—what's the trouble now?" demanded Tad.

"My burro. I go for him."

"You'll do nothing of the sort. You'll walk, or ride a pack animal," answered Stacy. "You don't deserve to have a burro."

"Here's his old burro now," called Walter, as a shambling object, much the worse for wear, came stumbling sleepily into camp.

The boys set up a shout that was quickly checked by Tad.

"If the burro can find the way what do you think an Indian could do, fellows?"

"That's right," agreed Professor Zepplin. "We had better keep quiet—"

"And hit the trail as fast as possible," added Tad. "Daylight must find us a long ways from here."

"And ride all night—is that what you mean?" complained Stacy.

"Yes; it'll give you an appetite for breakfast."

"I've got one already."

"That goes without saying," agreed Ned.

"Come, come, Juan!" urged Tad, observing that the guide was doing nothing more in the way of work than rubbing the nose of his prodigal burro. "Aren't you going to help us?"

"Yes; what do you think we're paying you good American dollars for?" demanded Ned.

"I think some of the Professor's hot drops would be good for what ails him," observed Stacy Brown. "I'll get the Professor to give him a dose right now."

"No, no, no! Juan no want fire drops."

"All right; get busy, then."

He did. Not since the last dose of the Professor's medicine had he shown such activity. Very soon after that the camp had been struck and the party was ready to take up its journey.

Tad took a last look about, to make sure that nothing had been left.

"I think I'll put out the fire," he said, tossing the bridle reins to Stacy, while he ran over to the dying camp-fire, whose embers he kicked apart, stamping them out one by one. "No use leaving a trail like that for any prowling redskin."

They were quickly under way after that, Juan leading the way without the least hesitancy. He and the burro worked together like a piece of automatic machinery.

"He might better walk and lead the burro," said Stacy, who had been observing their peculiar method of locomotion. "Should think it would be easier."

The moon was dropping slowly westward, and the party was using it for a guide, keeping the silver ball sharply to their right. Juan on the other hand had hitched his lazy chariot to a star.

By this star he was laying his course to the southward. The Pony Rider Boys enjoyed their moonlight trip immensely; and a gentle breeze from the desert drifting over them relieved the scorching heat of the late afternoon and early evening.

"Guess the Indians are not going to bother us," said Walter, riding up to Tad just before daylight.

"Probably not. They will be in too much trouble with the Government, after last night's performances, to give much thought to chasing us. And besides, I don't see why they should wish to do so. Had they been very anxious to be revenged on us, most likely they would not have allowed us to get away as they did."

"Was it very terrible, Tad?" asked Walter Perkins.

"What, the dance, or what happened afterwards?" laughed the lad.

"Both?"

"Well, I'm free to confess that neither was exactly pleasant. When they caught Chunky I thought it was all up with us. Hello. There's Mr. Daylight."

Glancing to the left the boys saw the sky turning to gray. A buzzard screamed overhead, laying its course for the mountains where it was journeying in search of food.

"What's that?" demanded Stacy, awakening from a doze in his saddle.

"Friend of yours with an appetite," grinned Ned.

"I thought it sounded like breakfast call," muttered Stacy, relapsing into sleep again, his head drooping forward until, a few minutes later, he was lying over the saddle pommel with arms thrown loosely about the pony's neck.

Ned, observing the lad's position, suddenly conceived a mischievous plan. Unnoticed by the others, he permitted his own pony to fall back until he was a short distance behind Stacy. The others were a little way ahead.

Ned rode slowly alongside his companion, as he passed, bringing the rowel of his spur sharply against the withers of Chunky's mount.

The effect was instantaneous.

The fat boy's mount, itself half asleep, suddenly humped its back, and with bunching feet leaped clear of the ground.

"Hello, what's the matter back there?" called Ned, who by this time was a full rod in advance of his companion.

Stacy did not answer. He was at that moment turning an undignified somersault in the air, his pony standing meekly, awaiting the next act in the little drama.

The fat boy landed on the plain in a heap.

"Are you hurt, Chunky?" cried Tad anxiously, slipping from his saddle and running to his companion.

"I—I dunno, I—I fell off, didn't I?"

"You're off, at least," grinned Ned. "What was the matter?"

"I—I dunno; do you?"

"How should I know? If you will go to sleep an a bucking broncho, you must expect things to happen."

Stacy, by this time, had scrambled to his feet; after which, he began a careful inventory of himself to make sure that he was all there. He grinned sheepishly.

Satisfying himself on this point, Stacy shrugged his shoulders and walked over to his pony with a suggestion of a limp.

"Now that we have halted we might as well make camp for a few hours, get breakfast and take a nap," suggested the Professor.

The boys welcomed this proposition gratefully, for they were beginning to feel the effects of their long night ride, added to which, two of them had had a series of trying experiences before starting out.

In the meantime, Stacy Brown had been examining his pony with more than usual care.

Tad observed his action, and wondered at it. A moment later, the fat boy having moved away; Tad thought he would take a look at the animal. He was curious to know what Stacy had in mind.

"So that's it, is it?" muttered Tad.

He found the mark of a spur on the pony's withers. While it had not punctured the skin, the spur had raked the coat, showing that the rowel had been applied with considerable force.

Tad, with a covert glance about, saw Ned Rector watching him.

"You're the guilty one, eh?" he demanded, walking up to Ned.

"S-h-h-h," cautioned Ned. "He'll be redheaded if he knows I am to blame for his coming a cropper."

"Chunky's not so slow as you might think. But that wasn't a nice thing to do. It's all right to play tricks, but I hope you won't be so cruel as to use a spur on a dumb animal, the way you did, even if he is an ill-tempered broncho. You might have broken Chunky's neck, too."

Ned's face flushed.

"It was a mean trick, I'll admit. Didn't strike me so at the time. Shall I ask Chunky's pardon?"

"Do as you think best. I should, were I in your place."

"Then, I will after breakfast."

Ned got busy at once, assisting to cook the morning meal, while Juan led the ponies out to a patch of grass and staked them down. While the Pony Rider cook was thus engaged, he felt a tug at his coat sleeve.

Turning sharply, Ned found Stacy at his side. Stacy's face was flushed and his eyes were snapping.

"What is it, Chunky?"

"Come over here, I want to talk with you."

They stepped off a few paces out of hearing of the others, Tad smiling to himself as he observed Stacy's act.

"Well, what's the matter, Chunky?"

"I can lick you, Ned Rector!"

"Wha—what?"

"Said I could lick you. Didn't say I was going to, understand. Just said I could—"

"Like to see you try it."

"All right; it's a go."

Ere Ned could recover from his surprise, Stacy Brown had launched himself upon his companion. One of Stacy's arms went about Ned's neck, one foot kicked a leg from under Ned, and the two lads went down in the dust together.

It had happened in a twinkling.

"Here, here! What's going on over there?" shouted the Professor, starting on a run, while the other lads were laughing.

Chunky was sitting on the chest of his fallen adversary, Ned struggling desperately to throw the lad off.

"Cock-a-doodle-doo!" crowed Chunky, in imitation of a rooster, flapping his hands on his thighs, in great good humor with himself.

Professor Zepplin grabbed him by the collar, jerking Stacy Brown from the fallen Pony Rider Boy.

Ned scrambled to his feet, and, with a sheepish grin on his face, proceeded to brush the dust from his clothes.

"Downed you, did he?" questioned Tad.

"It wasn't fair. I didn't know he was going to try."

"Neither did the Russians when the Japs sailed into them at Port Arthur," laughed Walter. "And they got what was coming to them."

"So did I. Chunky, I deserve more than you gave me. If you want to, beat me up some more."

"Now, isn't that sweet of him?" chortled Stacy. "I fell off my pony, then I fell on you, and we'll call it quits, eh, Ned?"

Ned put out a hand, which Stacy grasped with mock enthusiasm.

"We sure will."

"I'd like to know what this is all about?" questioned Walter. "Something's been going on."

"I made his pony throw him over," admitted Ned.

Stacy nodded with emphasis.

"He found it out and jumped on me."

"I'll turn you both over my knee if you try to repeat these performances," warned the Professor.

Linking arms, Stacy and Ned started for the breakfast table, humming,

"For he's a jolly good fellow,"

and a moment later all four of the lads were standing about the breakfast table, singing the chorus at the top of their voices.

CHAPTER VIII.
ASLEEP ON THE SLEEPY GRASS

The slanting rays of the sun got into the eyes of the Pony Rider Boys. Four arms were thrown over as many pairs of eyes to shut out the blinding light.

"Ho-ho-hum!" yawned Chunky.

Cocking an impish eye at his companions, he observed that each had fallen into a deep sleep again.

The fat boy cautiously gathered up a handful of dry sand and hurled it into the air. A shower of it sprinkled over them, into their eyes and half-opened mouths.

Three pairs of eyes were opened, then closed again.

Encouraged by his success, Stacy chuckled softly to himself, then dumped another handful of sand over his companions.

But he was not prepared for what followed.

Three muscular boys hurled themselves upon him. Instantly the peaceful scene was changed into a pandemonium of yells. Down came the tent poles, the canvas rising and falling as if imbued with sudden life.

Professor Zepplin, startled by the racket, roused himself and sprang from his own tent. Observing the erratic actions of the tent in which the boys had been sleeping, he instantly concluded that something serious had happened.

"Boys! boys!" he cried, running to the spot, frantically hauling away the canvas. "What has happened? What has happened?"

They were too busy to answer him. When finally he had uncovered what lay below, he found his charges literally tied up in a knot, rolling and tumbling, with Stacy Brown lying flat on his back, each of his three companions vigorously rubbing handfuls of sand over his face, down his neck and in the hair of his head.

"I think I'll take a hand in this myself," smiled the Professor. He ran to his tent, returning quickly. In his hands he carried two pails of water.

Unluckily for the boys, they had failed to observe what he was doing. Nor did they understand that they were in danger until the contents of the two pails had been dashed over them.

There were yells in earnest this time. The water turned the dirt into mud at once, and their faces were "sights." Stacy's face had been protected, in a measure, by the other boys who were bending over him rubbing in the sand.

The unexpected bath put a sudden end to their sport, and they staggered out shouting for vengeance. They did not even know who had been the cause of their undoing.

The Professor, as he walked away smiling, had handed the pails to the grinning Juan with instructions to refill them.

The unfortunate Juan, bearing the pails away, was the first person to catch the eyes of the lads, as they rubbed the sticky mud out of them.

With a howl they projected themselves upon him. Juan's grin changed instantly to an expression of great concern. He went down under their charge, with four boys, instead of three, on top of him.

"Duck him!" shouted some one.

"Yes! Douse him in the spring!" chorused the boys.

Juan cried out for the Professor, but his appeals were in vain.

Shouting in high glee the lads bore him to the spring from which they got their water. They plumped him in, not any too gently, again and again.

"Now roll him in the sand," suggested Ned.

They did so.

The wet clothing and body made the sand stick to him until the lazy Mexican was scarcely recognizable.

At this point Professor Zepplin took a hand. He came bounding to the scene and began throwing the boys roughly from their unhappy victim. Perhaps he was not greatly disturbed over the shaking up the guide had sustained, but of course he confided nothing of this to the boys.

"You ought to be ashamed of yourselves—for four of you to pitch on to one weak Mexican! I'm surprised, young gentlemen."

"But—but—he ducked us," protested Ned.

"He did nothing of the sort."

"What—didn't duck us? Guess I know water when I feel it," objected Walter.

"You were ducked, all right, but it is I, not Juan, who am responsible for that."

"You?" questioned the lads all at once.

The Professor nodded, a broad grin on his face.

"But he had the pails."

"I gave them to him, after pouring the water over you. That's what is known as circumstantial evidence, young gentlemen. Let it be a lesson to you to be careful how you convict anyone on that kind of evidence."

"Fellows," glowed Chunky, "we've made a mistake. Let's make it right by ducking the Professor."

The boys looked over Professor Zepplin critically.

"I guess we'd better defer that job till we grow some more," they decided, with a laugh.

The next fifteen minutes were fully occupied in cleaning up and putting on their clothes. They were all thoroughly awake now, with cheeks flushed and eyes sparkling after their violent exercise. The guide had rather sullenly washed off the wet dust that clung to his face and hands.

"Never mind the clothes, Juan," advised Ned. "It'll brush off as soon as it gets dry. We'll take up a contribution to buy you a clothes brush. Ever see one?"

Juan grinned.

"You promise not to gamble the money away if we give it to you?"

"Si."

"Shell out, fellows. Ten cents apiece. That ought to salve his injured feelings."

Ned passed the hat, all contributing.

"That makes forty cents. Here, Professor, you haven't put in your ten yet. It'll take just fifty cents to paste up Juan's injuries."

"That reminds me of a fellow I heard about once," announced Stacy.

"Are you going to tell a story?" questioned Ned.

"If you will keep still long enough," replied Stacy.

"Then me for the bunch grass. It's like going to a funeral to hear Chunky try to tell a story."

"Let him tell it," shouted the lads.

"Go on, Chunky. Never mind Ned. He'll laugh when he gets back to Chillicothe," jibed Walter.

"I heard of a fellow once—"

"Yes; you told us that before," jeered Ned.

"Not the one we ducked in the spring, was it?" grinned Tad.

"Who's telling this story?" demanded Stacy belligerently.

"You are, I guess. I won't interrupt again."

"Well, did I say this fellow was a boy?"

"No."

"Well, he was—he's grown up now. He rushed into a drug store—"

"Was anything chasing him?" asked Ned innocently.

Stacy gave no heed to the interruption.

"And he said to the man in the store, 'Please, sir, some liniment and some cement?'"

"'What?' asked the clerk all in a muddle. You see, he'd never had a prescription like that to fill before. It made him tired, 'cause he thought the kid was making fun of him."

"'What—what's the trouble? What do you want liniment and cement for?'

"'Cause,' said the boy to the pill man, ''cause mom hit pop on the head with a plate.'"

For a moment there was silence, then the boys roared. But Ned never smiled.

"Laugh, laugh! Why don't you laugh?" urged Walter.

"Laugh? Huh! I laughed myself almost sick over that a long time ago. Read it in an almanac when I was in short trousers."

"The ponies! The ponies!" cried Juan, rushing up to them, waving his arms, then running his fingers through his long black hair until it stood up like the quills of a porcupine.

"What!" queried the Pony Rider Boys in sudden alarm. "What's the matter with the ponies?"

Juan pointed to the place where the stock had been tethered after they arrived at the camp.

There was not an animal to be seen anywhere on the plain.

"Gone!" gasped the lads, with sinking hearts.

"No, no, no. There!" stammered the guide.

With one accord the boys ran at top speed to the spot indicated by Juan.

There, stretched out in the long grass lay bronchos and burros.

"They're dead, the ponies are dead, every one of them!" cried the lads aghast.

CHAPTER IX.
THE MIDNIGHT ALARM

"What's this, what's this?" demanded the Professor, striding up.

"Look! Look! The ponies are dead!" exclaimed Ned excitedly.

"What do you suppose could have happened to them?" stammered Walter.

"Is it possible? What's the meaning of this, guide?"

Juan shrugged his shoulders and showed his white teeth.

In the meantime Tad had hurried to his own pony, and was down on his knees examining it. Placing his hands on the animal's side, he remained in that position for an instant, then sprang up.

"They're not dead, fellows! They're alive!"

"Asleep," grumbled Ned disgustedly.

"But there's something the matter with them. Something has happened to the stock," added Tad.

"Only a false alarm," nodded Stacy.

"Think so? Try to wake your pony up," advised Tad.

Stacy had already hurried to his own broncho, and now began tugging at the bridle rein, with sundry pokes in the animal's ribs.

"I can't. He's in a trance," wailed Stacy, considerably startled.

That expression came nearer to describing the condition of the stock than any other words could have done.

"Guide, what do you know about this?" questioned the Professor. "Has some one been tampering with our animals?"

Juan shrugged his shoulders with an air of indifference.

"No bother bronchs."

"Then will you please tell us what is the matter with them?"

"*Sleepy grass!*"

"Sleepy grass?" chorused the lads.

"Of course they're asleep all right," added Ned. "But whoever heard of sleepy grass?"

"He means they're sleeping on the grass," Stacy informed them.

"Ah! I begin to understand," nodded the Professor. "I think I know what the trouble is now. The guide is no doubt right."

The boys gathered around him, all curiosity.

"Tell us about it, Professor. We are very much mystified?" said the Pony Riders.

"A long time ago I remember to have read, somewhere, of a certain grass in this region that possessed peculiar narcotic properties—"

"What's narcotic?" interrupted Stacy.

"Something that makes you go to sleep when you can't," explained Tad Butler, rather ambiguously.

"When eaten by horses or cattle it is said to put them into deep sleep. The Rockefeller Institute, I believe, is already making an analytical test of the grass."

"Please talk so I can understand it," begged Stacy.

"Yes; those words make my head ache," scowled Ned. "Even the guide is making up faces in his effort to understand."

"He does understand. He understands only too well. For many years this grass has been known. Cows turned out for the day would fail to return at night—"

"To be milked," interjected Stacy.

"And an investigation would disclose them sleeping in some region, where the sleepy grass grew

And the fat boy hummed:

"Down where the sleepy grass is growing."

"Travelers who have tied out their horses in patches of the grass for the night have been unable to continue their journey until the animals recovered from their strange sleep. Thus the properties of the grass became known."

"Indians use 'em to tame bad bronchos," the guide informed them.

"Just so."

"But, when will they wake up?" questioned Tad.

"Mebby sun-up to-morrow," answered Juan, glancing up at the sky.

"What, sleep twenty-four hours?" demanded Ned.

"Si."

"Preposterous."

"Then, then, we've got to remain here all the rest of the afternoon and night—is that it?" demanded Tad.

"It looks that way."

"And you knew about this stuff, Juan?" questioned Tad.

"Si."

"Well, you're a nice sort of a guide, I must say."

"You ought to be put off the reservation," threatened Stacy, shaking a menacing fist in front of the white teeth.

In the meantime, Tad had gone over to the animals again, and, taking them in turn, sought to stir them up. He found he could not do so. The ponies' heads would drop to the ground after he had lifted and let go of them, just as if the animals were dead.

"Gives you a creepy feeling, doesn't it?" shivered Walter.

"I should say it does," answered Ned.

"Well, what is it, Chunky?" asked Tad, who observed that Stacy had something on his mind that he was trying to formulate into words.

"I've got an idea, fellows," he exploded.

"Hold on to it, then. You may never get another," jeered Ned.

"What is it, Master Stacy?" asked the Professor.

"Then—then—then—that's what Juan and his burro have been eating all the time. I knew there was something the matter with them."

A loud laugh greeted the fat boy's suggestion.

"Guess he's about right, at that," grinned Tad.

"A brilliant thought," agreed the Professor. "Boys, I must have some of that grass. I shall make some experiments with it."

"Experiment on Chunky," they shouted.

"No; he sleeps quite well enough as it is," smiled the Professor.

"I want some of it too—no, not to eat," corrected the fat boy. "I'll feed it to my aunt's cat when I get back; then he won't be running away from home every night."

"Better unload the rest of the equipment, boys," advised the Professor. "If we must remain here all night we might as well make the best of it."

Without their ponies, the lads spent rather a restless afternoon. They had not fully realized before how much a part of them their horses had become until they were suddenly deprived of them.

In the meantime, the bronchos slept on undisturbed.

"I've got another idea," shouted Stacy.

"Keep it to yourself," growled Ned. "Your ideas, like your jokes, graduated a long time ago."

"Is there sleepy grass in the Catskill Mountains!" persisted Stacy.

"We don't know, and we don't—"

"I know there is, and that's what put Rip Van Winkle to sleep for twenty years," shouted the fat boy in high glee. "See, I know more than—"

"Yes; you're the original boy wonder. We'll take that for granted," nodded Ned Rector.

Tad, however, was not inclined to look upon their enforced delay with anything like amusement. To him it had its serious side. He had not forgotten that they had been fleeing from the Indians. When he got an opportunity to do so, without his companions overhearing, he approached the Professor.

"I think it would be a good plan for us to have a guard over our camp to-night."

"On account of?"

"Yes."

"Very well; I think myself that it would be a prudent move. Have Juan sit up, then."

"No, he's a sleepy bead. Suppose we boys take turns?"

"Very well; arrange it to suit yourselves. I presume we ought to do something of the sort every night. It might have saved us some trouble on our Ozark journey had we been that prudent. Arrange it to suit you. I'll take my turn."

"No; we can do it, Professor. You go to bed as usual. We'll draw lots to see who takes the different watches. With the four of us we'll have to take only two hours apiece. That won't be bad at all."

The other boys, after the plan had been explained to them, entered into it enthusiastically. Walter was to take the first trick, Ned the next, Chunky the third and Tad the fourth.

And they were to take their guns out with them. The Professor agreed to this, now that they had become more familiar with firearms. As a matter of fact, all the boys had developed into excellent marksmen, though Tad was recognized as the best shot of the party.

Professor Zepplin, during the afternoon, gave each of them a lesson in revolver shooting, using for the purpose, his heavy army revolver. They did pretty well with this weapon, but, of course, were not nearly as expert with it as with the rifle.

Evening came and the stock was still sleeping soundly. There was nothing the boys could do but let them sleep, though the fact of all the ponies and burros lying about as if dead began to make the Pony Riders nervous. Night came, and with it semi-darkness, the moon being overcast with a veil of fleecy white clouds, which cast a grayish film over the landscape. The lads joked each other about having the "creeps," but none would admit the charge.

Walter, with rifle slung over his right shoulder, went out on the first watch with instructions to go at least two hundred yards from camp and keep walking around the camp in a circle. This would protect them from surprises on all sides. Ned decided not to retire until he had taken his guard trick, in view of the fact that he was to go on at eleven o'clock. But Stacy, proposing to get all the sleep he was entitled to, turned in early. The rest did not disturb him. The boys were unusually quiet that evening, perhaps feeling that the responsibility of the safety of the camp rested wholly upon their youthful shoulders.

Ned came in at one o'clock, after having taken his turn, unslung his rifle, drew the cartridges then put them back in the magazine again.

"I might need them before morning," he told himself.

Chunky being sound asleep, Ned grabbed him by a foot giving him a violent pull.

"Wat'cher want? Get out!" growled the fat boy sleepily.

"Get up and take your watch!" commanded Ned.

"Who's afraid of Indians?" mumbled Stacy.

This time Ned took the lad by the collar, jerked him to his feet and shook him until Stacy yelled "Ouch!" so loudly as to awaken the entire camp.

It took some time, however, to get Stacy himself awake sufficiently to make him understand that he had a duty to perform. Finally, however, he shouldered his rifle, after surreptitiously helping himself to a sandwich from the cook tent. Then he marched off, munching the bread and meat.

"See here," snapped Ned, running after him. "You're not measuring off your distance. Come back and pace it off."

"How many?"

"Two hundred yards. Stretch your fat legs as far as they'll go, then you'll have a yard, more or less."

Stacy started all over again, forgot the count, came back, then tried it again. Even at that he was not sure whether he had gone one hundred yards or five.

He was awake enough, now, to observe his surroundings. The cool breezes of the night were tossing the leaves of the cottonwoods near the water course to the west of them, while here and there in the foliage might be heard the exultant notes of a mocking bird.

Stacy shivered.

"Guess it's going to freeze to-night," he decided, beginning his steady tramp about the camp of the Pony Rider Boys.

Muttering to himself, as was his habit when alone, Stacy kept on until finding himself opposite the ponies, he decided to go over and look at them. All were asleep. Not one had awakened since going down under the powerful influence of the "sleepy grass."

"I'd like to eat some of that stuff myself, right now," Chunky decided out loud. "I'd have a good excuse for going to sleep then. Now I can't without getting jumped on by the fellows. Wonder what time it is—only half-past one. Must be something the matter with my watch. I know I've been out more'n two hours."

This trip he circled out further from the camp, growing a little more confident because nothing had happened to disturb him.

In the meantime the camp slept in peace—that is, the lads did until nearly time for the change of guard. Then the whole party was aroused with the sudden, startling conviction that something serious had happened.

All at once the crack of a rifle sounded on the still night air. It was followed by another shot, and another, until four distinct reports had rolled across the plains.

In wild disorder the Pony Rider Boys tumbled from their cots, and, grasping their weapons, leaped from the tents.

"What's the row?" inquired the Professor.

"Wow! Wow! Wow! Yeow!" shrieked a shrill voice to the northward.

"It's Chunky. He's giving the alarm! We're attacked!" cried the lads.

Bang! Bang!

They saw the flash of the fat boy's weapon before the report reached their ears.

A moment later the other boys caught sight of Stacy dashing into camp, hatless, waving his rifle and yelling as if bereft of his senses.

"What is it? What is it?" cried the boys with one voice.

"Indians! Indians! The prairie's full of them!"

CHAPTER X.
MEETING THE ATTACK

Instantly the camp was thrown into confusion. The lads ran here and there, not knowing what to do.

"Get behind the ponies! That's the only cover we can find here. Run for it!"

And run they did, the Professor outdistancing all the rest in his attempt to secrete himself where the enemy's weapons would not be likely to reach him.

In a moment more, the camp of the Pony Rider Boys was deserted, and behind each sleeping pony lay a boy, with rifle barrel poked over the animal's back, ready to shoot at the first sign of the redskins. Stacy, in his excitement, had forgotten that not a cartridge was left in his magazine, and the others were too fully occupied to remember to tell him.

For all of half an hour did the party lie protected. The boys began to grow restive. Tad's suspicions were being slowly aroused.

"I'm going to do a little scouting," he told them, slipping from behind the pony and skulking along back of the tents. The moon was shining brightly now. He could see a long distance. Not a human being was in sight.

"I thought so," he muttered, retracing his steps. "See here, Stacy Brown, what did you see—what did you shoot at?" he demanded sternly.

"I—I shot the chute—I—I mean I chuted the shot—I mean—"

"Say, what do you mean?"

"I—I mean—say, leggo my neck, will you?" roared Chunky.

"Fellows, he doesn't know what he means."

"Guess he's been feeding on crazy grass out on the prairie," was Ned's conclusion.

"There isn't an Indian anywhere around here. I know it. They would have been after us long before this, if there had been."

One by one the boys came from their hiding places, the lazy Mexican last. Disapproving eyes were turned on Stacy.

"Chunky, you come along and show us where you were when you shot—did you shoot at an Indian?" asked Tad.

"Yes, and I—I—I shot him."

"Show us. We're all from Chillicothe," demanded Ned.

Stacy, with a show of importance, led the way, keeping a wary eye out for the enemy. It was noticed, however, that each of the lads held his rifle ready for business in case there should be an enemy about.

"There! I was standing right over there—I guess."

"You guess! Don't you know?" questioned the Professor.

"Yes; that's the place."

The lad walked over to the identical spot from which he had first fired his rifle.

"He was over there and I shot at him, so," said Stacy, leveling the weapon. "Ye-ow! There he is, now!" shrieked the boy.

Every weapon flashed up to a level with the eyes.

"There is something over there on the ground," decided the Professor.

"Put down your guns so you don't shoot me," said Tad. "I'm going to find out what it is."

Keeping his own weapon held at "ready," the lad walked boldly over to where a heap of some sort lay on the plain. It surely had not been there during the afternoon—Tad knew that.

He reached it, stooped, peered, then uttered a yell.

"What is it?" they cried, hurrying up.

"You've done it now, Chunky Brown. You certainly have gone and done it."

"What—what is it?" cried the others in alarm.

"You've shot the lazy Mexican's burro. That's your Indian, Stacy Brown."

Juan, who had followed them out on the plain, uttered a wail and threw himself upon the body of his prostrate burro. The animal, it seemed, had recovered consciousness during the night, and in a half-dazed condition had wandered out on the plain. Stacy, while crouching down on the ground, had seen the head and long ears of the burro. He thought the ears were part of the head dress of a savage and let fly a volley of bullets at it.

"He—he isn't dead," shouted the fat boy. "See, I just pinked him in the ears."

And, surely enough, an examination revealed a hole through each ear. The holes were so close to the animal's head that it was reasonable to suppose the shot had stunned him, being already in a weakened condition from the sleepy grass.

The boys set to work to rouse the burro, which they succeeded in doing in a short time. Juan, with arm around the lazy beast's neck, led it back to camp, petting and soothing it with a chattering that they could not understand.

There was no more sleep in camp that night, though the boys turned in at the Professor's suggestion. Every little while, laughter would sound in one of the tents, as the others fell to discussing Stacy's Indian attack.

The next morning they were overjoyed to find that the ponies had awakened and were trying to get up.

"Lead them out of that grass, fellows," shouted Tad, the moment he saw the ponies were coming around. "We don't want them to make another meal of that stuff."

"Nor take another of Chunky's Rip Van Winkle sleeps," added Ned.

Never having had a like experience, none of the lads knew what to do with their mounts after getting them sufficiently awake to lead them to a place of safety. They appealed to Juan for advice, but the lazy Mexican appeared to know even less than they.

Tad, after studying the question a few moments, decided to give them water, though sparingly. This they appeared to relish and braced up quite a little. But the boy would not allow them to graze until nearly noon, when each one took his pony out, making sure that there was none of the sleepy grass around. The animals were then permitted to graze.

About the middle of the afternoon Tad decided that all were fit to continue the journey, and that it would be safe to travel until sunset. Everyone was glad to get away from the spot where they had had such unpleasant experiences, and the boys set off, moving slowly, the stock not yet being in the best of condition.

Late in the afternoon, when they had about decided to make camp, one of the boys espied an object, something like a quarter of a mile away, that looked like the roof of a house.

Ned said it couldn't be that, as it appeared to be resting on the ground. They asked Juan if he knew what it was, and for a wonder he did. He said it was a dug-out—a place where a man lived.

"Is he a hermit?" asked Stacy apprehensively, at which there was a laugh. Stacy had not forgotten his experiences in the cave of the hermit of the Nevada Desert.

For the next hour, the lads were too busy, pitching tents and unloading the pack animals, to give further thought to the dug-out or its occupant; but when, after they had prepared their evening meal, they saw some one approaching on horseback, they were instantly curious again.

The newcomer proved to be the owner of the dug-out. He was a tall, square-jawed man, with a short, cropped iron-gray beard and small blue, twinkling eyes.

"Will you join us and have some supper?" asked Tad politely, walking out to greet the stranger.

"Thank you; I will, young man," smiled the stranger.

Tad introduced himself and companions.

"You probably have heard my name before, young men. It is Kris Kringle; I'm living out here for my health and doing a little ranching on the side."

Stacy looked his amazement.

"Is—is he Santa Claus?" he whispered, tugging at Tad's coat sleeve.

"No, young man. I am not related to the gentleman you refer to," grinned Mr. Kringle.

There was a general laugh at Stacy's expense.

After supper, the visitor invited all hands to ride over to his dug-out and spend the evening with him. The boys accepted gladly, never having seen the inside of a dug-out, and not knowing what one looked like. Professor Zepplin had taken a sudden liking to the man with the Christmas name, and soon the two were engaged in earnest conversation.

The distance being so short, Tad decided that they had better walk, leaving the ponies in charge of Juan so they might get a full night's rest. Then all hands set out for the dug-out.

A short flight of steps led down into the place, the roof of which was raised just far enough above the ground to permit of two narrow windows on each side and at the rear end.

The room in which they found themselves, proved to be a combination kitchen and dining room. Its neatness and orderliness impressed them at once.

"And here," said Kris Kringle, "is what I call my den," throwing open a door leading into a rear room and lighting a hanging oil lamp.

The Pony Rider Boys uttered an exclamation of surprised delight.

On a hardwood floor lay a profusion of brightly colored Navajo rugs, the walls being hung with others of exquisite workmanship and coloring, interspersed with weapons and trophies of the chase, while in other parts of the room were rare specimens of pottery from ancient adobe houses of the Pueblos.

At the far end of the room was a great fire-place. Book cases, home-made, stood about the room, full of books. The Professor realized, at once, that they were in the home of a student and a collector.

"This is indeed an oasis in the desert," he glowed. "I shall be loath to leave here."

"Then don't," smiled Mr. Kringle. "I'm sure I am glad enough to have company. Seldom ever see anyone here, except now and then a roving band of Indians."

"Indians!" exclaimed Tad. "Do you have any trouble with them?"

"Well, they know better than to bother with me much. We have had an occasional argument," said their host, his jaws setting almost stubbornly for the instant. "Most of the tribes in the state are peaceful, though the Apaches are as bad as ever. They behave themselves because they have to, not because they wish to do so."

"I saw their fire dance the other night," began Tad.

"What?" demanded Mr. Kringle.

"Fire dance."

"Tell me about it?"

Tad did so, the host listening with grave face until the recital was ended.

He shook his head disapprovingly.

"And this—this Indian that you knocked down—was he an Apache?"

"I don't know. I think so, though. He had on a peculiar head dress

"That was one of them," interrupted Mr. Kringle, with emphasis. "And I'll wager you haven't heard the last of him yet. That's an insult which the Apache brave will harbor under his copper skin forever. He'll wait for years, but he'll get even if he can."

The faces of the Pony Rider Boys were grave.

"Have you a reliable guide?"

"Far from it," answered the Professor. "If I knew where I could get another, I'd pack him off without ceremony."

Kris Kringle was silent for a moment.

"I need a little change of scene," he smiled. "How would you like to have me take the trail with you for a week or so?"

"Would you?" glowed the Professor, half rising from his chair.

"I think I might."

"Hurrah!" cried the Pony Riders enthusiastically. "That will be fine."

"Of course, you understand that I expect no pay. I am going because I happen to take a notion to do so. Perhaps I'll be able to serve you at the same time."

The Professor grasped Mr. Kringle by the hand impulsively.

"I'll send that lazy Juan on his way this very night—"

"Let me do it," interposed Stacy, with flushing face. "I'll do it right, Professor. But I'll put on my pair of heavy boots first, so it'll hurt him more."

The boys shouted with laughter, while the new guide's eyes twinkled merrily.

"I think, perhaps, the young man might do it even more effectively than you or I," he said. "Have you weapons, Professor?"

"Rifles."

"That's good. We may need them."

"Then you think?"

"One can never tell."

CHAPTER XI.
RIDING WITH KRIS KRINGLE

A slender ribbon of dust unrolling across the plain far to the northward marked the receding trail of Juan and his lazy burro. They had given him a week's extra pay and sent him on his way.

The burro was making for home, aided by the busy feet of its master, while Stacy Brown, shading his eyes with one hand, was watching the progress of the guide, whom he had just sent adrift.

"Well, he's gone," grinned Stacy, turning to his companions, who were busy striking camp.

"And a good riddance," nodded Tad.

"He'll probably join the Indians and tell them where we are," suggested Walter.

"I hadn't thought of that," replied Tad. "Still, if they wish to find us they know how without Juan's telling them."

"How?"

"They can follow a trail with their eyes shut," said Ned.

"That's right. They do not need to be told," muttered Tad.

Everything being in readiness, the boys started with their outfit for the dug-out, where they were to be joined by Kris Kringle. They felt a real relief to know that they were to have with them a strong man on whom they were sure they could rely to do the right thing under all circumstances. Tad, however, believed that Mr. Kringle had decided to join them, fearing they would be attacked by the Apaches and come to serious harm. Yet he hardly thought the redskins would dare to follow them, after the latter had once gotten over the frenzy of their fire dance. By that time the Indian agents would have rounded them all up on the reservations, where the Indians would be able to do no more harm for a while.

After picking up the new guide the start was made. The party had water in plenty in the water-bags, so that no effort was made to pick up a water hole when they made camp late in the afternoon. The guide had brought in his pack a tough old sage hen, at which the lads were inclined to jeer when he announced his intention of cooking it for their supper.

"You'll change your mind when you taste it, young gentlemen. It depends upon the cooking entirely. A sage hen may be a delicious morsel, or it may not," answered Mr. Kringle, with a grin.

They were encamped near a succession of low-lying buttes, and to while away the time until the supper hour, the boys strolled away singly to stretch their legs on the plain after the long day's ride in the hot sun.

When they returned an hour or so later, Stacy, they observed, was swinging a curious forked stick that he had picked up somewhere a few moments ago.

"What you got there?" questioned Ned.

"Don't know. Picked it up on the plain. Such a funny looking thing, that I brought it along."

"Let me see it," asked Mr. Kringle.

Stacy handed it to him.

"This," said the guide, turning the stick over in his hand, "is a divining rod."

"Divining rod?" demanded Stacy, pressing forward.

"Yes."

"Never heard of it. Is it good to eat?"

"Looks to me like a wish bone," interjected Ned. "Do you eat wish bones, Chunky?"

"Might, if I were hungry enough."

"A divining rod is used to locate springs. Some users of it have been very successful. I couldn't find a lake with it, even if I fell in first."

"Indeed," marveled the Professor. "I have heard of the remarkable work of divining rods. What Rind of wood is it?"

"This is hazel wood. Oak, elm, ash or privet also are used, but hazel is preferred in this country."

"Then—then we won't have to go dry any more—I can find water with this when I'm dry?" questioned Stacy.

"You might; then again you might not."

"Better take it away from him," suggested Ned. "He might find a spring. If he did he'd be sure to fall in and drown."

The stick, which was shaped like the letter Y, was an object of great interest to the Pony Rider Boys. One by one they took it out on the plain, in an effort to locate some water. The guide instructed them to hold the Y with the bottom up, one prong in each hand and to walk slowly.

But, try as they would, they were able to get no results.

"The thing's a fraud!" exclaimed Ned disgustedly, throwing the divining rod away.

Stacy picked it up.

"I know why it doesn't work," he said.

"Why?" demanded the other boys.

"'Cause—'cause there isn't any water to make it work," he replied wisely.

The boys groaned.

Shortly after returning to camp, they found the fat boy standing over a pail of water holding the stick above it.

He was talking to the stick confidentially, urging it to "do something," to the intense amusement of the whole outfit.

"Now, where's your theory?" questioned the Professor.

"Why, it doesn't have to work, does it? Don't we know there's water here? If we didn't the stick would tell us, maybe. Take my word for it, this outfit won't have to go dry after this. Stacy Brown and his magic wand will find all the water needed," continued the fat boy proudly.

"Your logic is good, at any rate, even if the rod doesn't work at command," laughed the Professor.

Supper was a jolly affair, for everyone was in high spirits. The sage hen, contrary to general expectation, was found to be delicious.

Chunky begged for the wish bone and got it. He said he'd use it for a divining rod when he wanted to find a little spring.

"Mr. Kringle, I am commissioned by the fellows to ask you a question," announced Tad, after the meal had been in progress for a time.

"Ask it," smiled the guide.

"We thought we'd like to call you Santa Claus, seeing you've brought us so much cheer. Then again, it's your name you know. Kris Kringle is Santa Claus."

"Oh, well, call me what you please, young men."

From that moment on, Kris Kringle was Santa Claus to the Pony Rider Boys.

They had now come to a rolling country, with here and there high buttes, followed by large areas of bottom lands which were covered with rank growths of bunch grass. Traveling was more difficult than it had been, and water more scarce.

It was on the second day out, after they had been skirmishing for water in every direction, that the lads heard the familiar yell from Chunky.

"There goes the trouble maker," cried Ned. "He's at it again."

The guide bounded up, starting on a run for the spot where Chunky's wail had been heard. The others were not far behind.

They saw the red, perspiring face of the fat boy above a clump of grass, his yells for help continuing, unabated.

"What is it?" shouted the guide.

"I've got it, Santa Claus! I've got it!"

"Got what?" roared the Professor.

"The stick!—I mean it's got me. Help! Help!"

Stacy was wrestling about as if engaged in combat with some enemy. They could not imagine what had gone wrong—what had caused his sudden cries of alarm.

"It's the divining rod!" called the guide.

"He's found water!" shouted the boys.

"I've got it! I've got it! Come help me hold it. The thing's jerking my arms off."

To the amazement of the Pony Rider Boys, the forked stick in the hands of the fat boy was performing some strange antics. Breathing hard, he would force it up until it was nearly upright, when all at once the point of the triangle would suddenly swerve downward, bending the rod almost to the breaking point.

"See it? See it?"

"Most remarkable," breathed Professor Zepplin.

"Yes, there can be no doubt about it," nodded the guide.

"He's bluffing," disagreed Ned.

"Doesn't look to me as if he were," returned Tad.

"Take hold with me here, if you don't believe me," cried Stacy. "No, not on the stick, take hold of my wrists."

Ned promptly accepted the invitation.

Instantly the tug of the divining rod was felt by the new hands.

Ned let go quickly.

"Ugh! The thing gives me the creeps."

"Let me try it, Master Stacy," said Professor Zepplin.

"I can't let go of it," wailed Chunky.

"Step off a piece," directed the guide.

Stacy did so, whereupon the divining rod immediately ceased its peculiar actions.

The Professor took hold of it, but the rod refused to work for him.

"Let Santa Claus try it," suggested Ned.

The guide did so, but with no more success than the Professor had had.

"I told you it wouldn't work for me," Mr. Kringle grinned. "Here, Master Tad, you try it."

Tad, with the rod grasped firmly in his hands, walked back and forth three times without result. On the fourth attempt, however, the stick suddenly bent nearly double.

All were amazed.

"Why were we unable to get results, Mr. Kringle?" questioned the Professor.

"According to some French writers as much depends upon the man as on the divining rod. Where one succeeds another fails absolutely. Supposing the others take a try?"

Walter and Ned did so, but neither could get the rod to move for him.

"I guess Chunky is the champion water-finder," laughed Ned.

"Would it not be a good idea to find out whether or not there *is* water here?" asked the Professor.

"Yes," agreed the guide. "It may be so far down that we cannot reach it, however. You know in some parts of this region they are locating water with the rod and sinking artesian wells."

"Why—why didn't we think to bring some down with us?" demanded Chunky. "Can't we get any in some of the towns down here?"

"Some what?" questioned the guide.

"Artesian wells."

A roar greeted the fat boy's question.

"Bring down a load of artesian wells!" jeered Ned.

"An artesian well, my boy, is nothing more than a hole in the ground," the guide informed him, much to Chunky's chagrin.

The spot where the divining rod had so suddenly gotten busy was about midway of an old water course, covered with a thick growth of bunch grass.

"Get some tools, boys," directed the Professor.

Tad ran back to camp, which lay some distance to the east of where they were gathered. Searching out a pick and two shovels, he leaped on his pony, dashing back to the arroyo.

"That was quickly done," smiled Santa Claus. "Are all of you lads as quick on an errand as that?"

"Only Chunky," answered Ned solemnly.

The guide began to dig, in which effort he was joined by Stacy Brown, who, with a shovel, caved in about as much dirt as he threw out.

"Here, give me that shovel," commanded Ned. "You'll fill up the bole before we get it dug."

Tad, having tethered his pony, took the extra shovel and went to work.

"Guess it's a false alarm," decided Ned, after they were up to their shoulders in the hole.

"Don't be too sure. The ground is quite damp here. Try your rod, young man."

"Chunky held the divining rod over the excavation, whereupon it drew down with even greater force than before.

"Dig," directed the guide.

They did so with a will.

"Here's water!" shouted Kris Kringle.

They crowded about the hole, amazement written on every face.

A fresh, cool stream bubbled up into the hole, causing those in the pit to scramble out hastily.

"Some of you boys run back to camp and fetch pails and water-bags," directed the guide.

"I'll go. I've got the pony here," spoke up Tad.

"No; I want you to do something else for me."

"We'll all go," offered Walter. The three lads started on a run, Chunky holding his precious divining rod tightly clasped in both hands.

"What is it you wish?" questioned Tad.

"I wish you would ride over toward that small butte and cut a load of brush. Want to rip-rap the outer edge of this water hole, so the bank will not cave in and undo all our work! Have you a hatchet?"

"Yes, in my saddlebags."

"Good. Hurry, please."

Tad leaped into the saddle, and putting spurs to his broncho, tore through the high bunch grass, above which only his head was now observable. In a short time he was back with the green stuff piled high on the saddle in front of him, with a large bundle tied to the cantle of the saddle behind.

Unloading this, Butler started back at a gallop for more. When there was work to be done, Tad Butler was happy. Activity to him was a tonic that spurred him on to ever greater efforts.

This time he found himself obliged to climb higher up the butte in order to get branches of available size. These he cut and threw down. After having procured what he thought would be all he could carry the lad scrambled down, and, dropping on his knees began tying them into bundles. The heat was sweltering, and occasionally be paused to wipe away the perspiration.

"I smell smoke," sniffed Tad. "I wonder where it comes from?"

The odor grew stronger, but so interested was he in his labor that he did not at once understand the significance of his discovery.

"W-h-o-o-e-e!"

It was a long-drawn, warning shout.

"It's a signal!" exclaimed the lad, straightening up. "I wonder what's the matter?"

As he looked toward the camp a great wall of flame seemed to leap from the ground between him and his companions. There it poised for one brief instant, then, with a roar swooped down into the tall bunch grass, rushing roaring and crackling toward him.

For an instant he stood unbelieving, then the truth dawned upon him.

"The prairie's on fire!" cried Tad.

CHAPTER XII.
THE DASH FOR LIFE

The shouts of the Pony Rider Boys and of the guide were swallowed up in the roar of the flames.

"They'll be burned alive!" whispered the lad.

Then, all at once he realized that he himself was in dire peril.

"I'll have to go the other way and be quick about it at that," he decided, making a dash for the pony, that already was whinnying with fear and tugging at its tether.

Tad did not wait to untie the stake rope. With a sweep of his knife he severed it and vaulted into the saddle.

Whirling the animal about he headed to the west. To his alarm he suddenly discovered that the prairie fire was rapidly encircling him, the flames running around the outer edge of the bottoms with express train speed, threatening to head him off and envelop him. Had it not been for the long grass, which, tangling the feet of the pony, made full speed impossible, the race with the flames would have been an easy one to win. As it was, Tad knew that the chances were against him.

But the dire peril in which he found himself did not daunt the Pony Rider Boy. Perhaps his face had grown a shade paler underneath the tan, but that was all. His senses were on the alert, his lips met in a firm pressure and the hand gripped the bridle rein a little more firmly, perhaps, than usual.

Uttering a shrill cry to inform his companions that he was alive to his peril, and at the same time to encourage the broncho, Tad dug in the rowels of his spurs.

The frightened pony cleared the ground with all four feet, uttering a squeal, and launching itself at the rapidly narrowing clear space ahead of him; and urged to greater and greater endeavor at every leap by the short, sharp "yips" of his rider.

For all the concern that showed in his face, Tad Butler might have been running a horse race for a prize rather than fleeing for his life.

"If I make it I'm lucky,"—commented Tad grimly. He found himself wondering, at the same time, how the fire had started. He knew that the flames first showed themselves midway between where he was at work and the place where his companions were engaged at the water hole.

He could not understand it. Fire was necessary to use to start fire, and he knew that none of them had been foolish enough even to light a match in the dry bunch grass of the prairie.

The flames were reaching mountain high by this time, great clouds of smoke rolling in on the breeze and nearly suffocating him.

At times Tad was unable to see the opening ahead of him. When, however, the smoke lifted, giving him a momentary view, he saw that the gap was rapidly closing.

All at once his attention was drawn from the closing gap.

"Yeow! Yeow! Yeow! Y-e-o-w!"

A series of shrill, blood curdling yells from out the pall of smoke and flame at the rear, bombarded his ears.

At first he thought it was Indians; then the improbability of this being the case came to him.

"Yeow! Yeow! Yeow!" persisted the voice behind, and it was coming nearer every second.

Tad slackened the speed of his pony ever so little, despite the peril of his position.

"There's somebody in there behind me, and, he'll never get out alive if he loses his way."

The moment this thought occurred to him, Tad began to yell at the top of his voice.

Suddenly from out the thick veil of smoke burst a pony with a mighty snort, coming on in bounds, each one of which cleared many feet of ground. On the pony's back was Stacy Brown, hatless, coatless, his hair standing up in the breeze, his face as red as if it had come in actual contact with the flames.

"Yeow!" he roared, as his pony shot past Tad as if the latter's mount were standing still. Where Stacy had come from, how he had passed through that wall of flame, Tad had not the slightest idea.

As a matter of fact the explanation was simple enough. The guide had sent Chunky out to assist Tad in bringing in the rip-rapping material. Stacy had made a detour from the camp, having gotten just inside the danger zone when the fire broke out. Guided by the butte where he knew his companion must be, Stacy headed for that point. There he came upon Tad's trail, and began yelling to attract his attention. He had heard Tad's answering cry, and this inspired the fat boy to renewed efforts.

Stacy, now that he had passed Tad, slowed up ever so little. He had passed his companion so swiftly that he was unable to determine whether or not Tad were in distress.

The latter came up, overhauling Stacy in a few moments. Both ponies were steaming from the terrific gruelling they were giving themselves.

"What you doing here?" exploded Tad.

"Same thing you are."

"What do you mean?"

"Trying to save myself from being burned alive—"

"Don't slow up! Don't slow up!" shouted Tad. "Keep going!"

"I am. Wat's matter with you?"

"I don't see what you had to come tumbling into this mess for," objected Tad.

"Didn't tumble in. Rode in. Came to help you—"

"Precious lot of help you'll be to me. Lucky if we're not both burned with our boots on. See! The flame's narrowing in on us. More steam, Chunky! More steam!" urged Tad.

"Can't. Blow up the boiler if I do," Stacy could not be other than humorous, even under their present trying situation.

"That's better than burning out your fires, and it's quicker too—"

All at once, Chunky uttered a terrible howl. His pony had stepped into a hole and gone down floundering in the long grass, Chunky himself having been hurled over the animal's head, landing several feet in advance.

"Help! Help!"

The rest was lost as the fat boy's face plowed the earth filling mouth, eyes and nostrils.

Tad did not lose his presence of mind, though events had been following each other in such quick succession.

Changing the reins to his right hand and bunching them there, he grasped the pommel of the saddle, driving his own pony straight at the kicking, floundering Chunky.

The pony swerved ever so little, Tad's body swept down, and when it rose, his fingers were fastened in the shirt collar of his companion, with Chunky yelling and choking, as he was being dragged over the ground at almost a killing pace.

Tad had no time to do more than hold on to his friend. He dared not stop to lift him to the saddle just then. The flames were roaring behind them and on either side, leaving a long, narrow lane ahead, through which lay their only hope of safety.

"Buck up! Buck up, Chunky!" shouted Tad, himself taking a fresh brace in the stirrups, for the weight of the fat boy's dragging body was slowly pulling Tad from the saddle.

Stacy was howling like an Indian, not from fear, but from anger at the rough usage to which he was being subjected. He did not stop to think that it was the only way his life might be saved—nor that his own pony lay back there in the bunch grass amid the flame and smoke.

Tad knew it.

Now, by a mighty effort Tad righted himself again, and, leaning forward, threw one arm about the pony's neck, trusting to the animal to follow the outward trail to safety of its own accord.

Tad felt a sudden jolt that nearly caused him to slide from his pony on the side opposite Chunky. At the same time, the strain on the lad's arm was suddenly released.

Tad was up on his saddle like a flash. His right hand held the fat boy's shirt, while a series of howls to the rear told him where the owner of the shirt lay.

Tad groaned. Pulling his pony fairly back on its haunches, he dashed back where Stacy lay kicking, entangling himself deeper and deeper in the bunch grass.

Had Tad not had presence of mind they both might have perished right there. He was off like a flash. With supreme strength, he grasped the body of his fallen companion, raising him into the saddle.

"Hold on!" he shouted. "Don't you dare fall off!"

Stacy clung like a monkey to a pony in a circus race.

"Y-i-i-p!" trilled Tad. He had no time to mount. Already he could feel the hot breath of the flames on his cheek.

The broncho was off with a bound.

"Tad! Tad!" cried Chunky in sudden alarm, now realizing that he was alone. "Whe—where are you?"

"H-h-h-h-e-r-e!"

"W-w-where?"

"H-h-h-holding to the b-r-r-oncho's t-tail."

"Wow!" howled Stacy, as, turning in the saddle, he discovered his companion being fairly jerked through the air, holding fast to the pony's tail, the lad's feet hardly touching the ground at all. The broncho, that ordinarily would have resented such treatment, too fully occupied in saving his own life from the flames, gave no heed to the weight he was dragging, and it is doubtful if he even realized there was any additional weight there.

With a final, desperate leap, the broncho shot out ahead of the narrowing lane. Like the jaws of some great monster, the two lapping lines of fire closed in behind them, roaring as if with deadly rage.

The pony dashed out into a broad, open water course, whose dry, glistening sands would prove an effectual barrier to the prairie fire.

Tad, though everything was swimming before his eyes, realized quickly that they were now well out of danger.

"St-t-t-top him. I c-c-c-an't let go if you d-d-don't."

"Whoa! Whoa! Don't you know enough to quit when you're through?" chided Chunky, tugging at the reins. The broncho carried them some distance before the lad was able to pull him down. Finally he did so.

"Leggo!" he shouted, at the same time whirling the pony sharply about, fairly "cracking the whip" with Tad Butler.

Chunky's clever foresight probably saved Tad Butler's life, for, instantly the pony found itself free, it began bucking and kicking in a circle, kicking a ring all round the compass before it finally decided to settle down on all fours. Finishing, it meekly lowered its nose to the ground and now, as docile as a kitten after having supped on warm milk, began dozing, the steam rising in a cloud from its sides.

"Well, of all the fool fools, you're the champion fool!" growled Stacy, slipping from the saddle and surveying the broncho with disapproving eyes. "Hah! I guess we'd been done to a turn by this if it hadn't been for you, just the same. Hello, Tad!"

Tad had doubled up in a heap where the tail of the broncho had flung him. He was well-nigh spent, but he smiled back at his companion, who stood on a slight rise of ground, almost a heroic figure.

Chunky's shirt was entirely missing, his skin red from the heat, ridged with scratches where he had come in violent contact with cactus plants, his hair tousled and gray with dust.

"Well you are a sight," grinned Tad.

"You wouldn't take a prize at a baby show yourself," retorted Stacy, spicily.

Tad's clothes were torn, and his limbs were black and blue all the way down where the hoofs of the broncho had raked them again and again.

"My arms feel a foot longer than they did. What are you looking at?"

Stacy's eyes grew large and luminous as he gazed off over the plains.

"Look! Look, Tad!" he whispered.

CHAPTER XIII.
FOLLOWING A HOT TRAIL

"Fire! Fire!" cried Professor Zepplin, leaping up from where he had been leaning over, watching the water bubbling in the bottom of the excavation they had made.

The guide had been hanging over the hole, dipping water to Ned, who was turning it into the water-bags.

"Where, where?" demanded Mr. Kringle explosively. He also sprang to his feet. "It's a prairie fire!"

"The boys are caught. They'll perish!" exclaimed Professor Zepplin, with blanching face. "Go to them, go to them, Mr. Kringle!" he begged.

"No living thing could get through that wall of fire, Professor," announced the guide impressively. "We'll shout and perhaps, if alive, they'll bear us."

They did so, with the result already known.

"Which direction did Master Stacy take?" Mr. Kringle asked.

"I saw him riding down that way," replied Walter, pointing excitedly.

"Then, perhaps he is safe outside of the fire zone. Some of you hurry back to the camp, The stock may take fright and stampede. No, we'll all go. The wind may shift at any moment, and while I do not think the flames could reach the camp, all our animals might be suffocated, even if they did not succeed in getting away."

"But you're not going to desert Tad and Chunky, are you?" demanded Walter indignantly.

"Certainly not. What can we do here? We must get the ponies first; then we'll hurry to them. I'm afraid they've been caught," answered the guide.

"If there's any way of escape you may depend upon it that Master Tad has discovered that way," answered the Professor. "He is a resourceful boy, and—"

But the rest were already dashing madly toward the camp and Professor Zepplin began to do so with all speed to catch up with them. The hot breath of the prairie fire had brought the color to his blanched cheeks.

"How—how do you think the fire started?" stammered the Professor, when he at last came up with the guide.

"It was set afire," answered Kris Kringle grimly.

"Set!" shouted the Professor and the two boys all in one breath.

"Yes."

"By whom?"

"That remains to be seen."

"Do you mean that one of the boys was imprudent enough to build a fire in that grass? Surely they would not have been so foolish as to do a thing like that."

"As I said, that remains to be seen. The first thing to be done is to get to them as quickly as possible, though I don't know that we can do any good. They're either out of it, by this time, or else they're not," added Mr. Kringle suggestively. "Professor, I wish you and one of the boys would get out your rifles, mount your ponies and watch the camp, while two of us go in search of the lost ones."

"Watch the camp?"

"Yes."

"For what reason?"

"Merely as a precaution."

"I'll attend to that. I want all of you to get after Tad and Stacy. We don't care about the camp particularly, when compared with two human lives."

The smoke was rolling over them in such dense clouds that the camp was wholly obscured from view until they were upon it.

"Quick! Get the horses before they break away!" commanded the guide.

"I can't find them!" shouted Ned, who had bounded on ahead and disappeared in the great suffocating cloud.

Walter was only a few steps behind him, both boys groping, blinking and coughing as the smoke got into eyes and lungs.

"Lie down when it gets stronger than you can stand. There's always a current of fresh air near the ground," called the guide.

Both lads adopted his suggestion instantly, and they were none too soon, for already they were getting dizzy. After a few long breaths, they were up, groping about once more in search of the stock.

"Over to you right," called the Professor.

"We've been there. They're not there at all," answered Ned.

By this time the guide had dived into the cloud.

"The stock has gone," they heard him shoat.

"Have they stampeded?" roared the Professor.

"I don't know. I'll find out in a minute."

"Queer that this smoke blows two ways at once," said Walter.

"There is a slight breeze blowing this way," explained Ned. "Not enough, however, to turn the fire back. It has got too good a start."

Suddenly a weird "c-o-o-e-e" sounded to the right of them.

"What's that?"

"It's the guide, Walt. He's trying to call the boys, to see if they are alive," explained Ned.

"I don't think so. That cry is for some other purpose. I'm going over where he is to find out what it does mean. Come on."

Together the lads ran as fast as they could in the direction from which the guide's voice had come.

They found him with hands shaped into a megaphone, uttering his shrill cries. He made no answer to their questions as to what he was trying to do.

All at once off in the cloud they heard rapid hoofbeats. The boys glanced at each other in surprise.

"It's the ponies returning," breathed Walter Perkins.

Ned shook his head.

The cries now took on a more insistent tone, and a moment later two ponies came whinnying into the camp, snorting with fear. Kris Kringle spoke to them sharply, whereupon they came trotting up to him with every evidence of pleasure.

The lads were amazed.

"Can you boys shoot a rope?"

"Yes," they answered together.

"Which one is the better at it?"

"Ned is more expert than I am."

"Take one of my ponies. We've got to go after the stock. Rope and bring them in as fast as possible. It's getting late, and it will be dark before we know it. There's not more than two hours of daylight left."

"I can take my pony and help," began Walter.

"You haven't any pony. They're all gone."

Ned and the guide dashed from the camp at break-neck speed. Emerging from the dust cloud they saw some of the stock far off on the plain.

"There they are!" cried Ned

"Thank goodness, they're all together. And they are not running. We've got them bunched."

"Were they afraid of the smoke? What made them break away?"

"They didn't break away."

"What?"

"Their tethers were cut and they were sent adrift," answered the guide grimly.

Ned was speechless with surprise.

Some of the ponies, objecting to being roped, ran away, necessitating a lively chase. Kris Kringle worked with the precision of an automatic gun and with proportionate speed. In half an hour they had roped all the ponies, and, with the burros trailing along behind, started back to camp as rapidly as possible.

A heavy pall of smoke still hung over the camp and all the surrounding country.

Once more they staked down the ponies and pack animals, and urging vigilance on the part of Professor Zepplin, Ned and the guide dashed away at full gallop in search of the two missing lads.

"Are we going through the fire?" questioned Ned apprehensively.

"We're going to try it. The worst of it must have passed before this, but we may have to turn back or turn out for spots. It's the shortest way, and the only course to follow if we want to know what has become of them."

Spreading out a little they continued on their way, the ponies snorting, threatening to whirl about and race back into the open plain. The ground was like a furnace and the grass smouldered beneath them, heating their feet and singeing their fetlocks.

Suddenly Ned's pony reared into the air, bucked and hurled its rider far over into the smouldering bunch grass.

Ned uttered a yell of warning as he felt himself going.

The guide wheeled like a flash. Ned's mount had whirled and was away like a shot. But the guide was after him with even greater speed. The chase came to an abrupt ending some few rods farther on, when Kris Kringle's lariat squirmed out, bringing the fleeing pony to the ground with its nose in the hot dust.

Without dismounting, the guide turned his own mount, and fairly dragging the unwilling pony behind him, pounded back to the place where Ned had been unhorsed.

"Grab him!" commanded the guide to Ned, who had quickly scrambled to his feet. "What was it that he saw?"

"I don't know. Guess he made up his mind to go back."

"No; he saw something. Hang on to him and cover the ground all about you till you find it."

"Wha—what do you—"

"Never mind. Look!"

"Here! Here it is!" cried Ned aghast.

The guide was at his side instantly.

"It's a pony," gasped the Pony Rider boy.

Kris Kringle was off his own mount instantly, and bidding Ned hold the animal, he made a brief examination of the fallen horse, after which he darted here and there, unheeding the fact that the still burning grass was blistering his feet through the heavy soles of his boots.

For several rods Kringle ran along the faint trail that Tad and Stacy had left, or rather, that the fire had left after passing over it.

"They beat their way out here. We may find them later. Come on!"

Again Ned and the guide dashed away, both keeping their gaze on the smoking prairie about them. The smoke now was almost more than they could bear.

"Do—do you think they are alive?" asked Ned unsteadily.

"So far. If they are not, it's not their fault. The Professor is right. Those boys have pluck enough to pull them through, but sometimes pluck alone will not do it. A prairie fire is no respecter of pluck."

They burst out into an open space. There were no signs of either of the missing boys.

"Something has happened to them. We must have missed them," announced the guide.

CHAPTER XIV.
AGAINST BIG ODDS

"What is it, Chunky?"

"There!"

Tad jerked his companion flat on the ground, flattening himself beside Stacy at the same instant.

What had caused their sudden alarm was the sight of two Indians, sitting on their ponies without saddles, some distance out on the open plain. The redskins were wrapped in their brightly colored blankets, which enveloped them from head to knees. Even the hands were invisible beneath the folds of the blankets.

"D-d-do you think they saw us, Tad?"

"I don't know. It's safe to say they did. Indian eyes don't miss very much. You ought to know that, by this time. I wish we could make that pony lie down."

"Why don't you?"

"He's too afraid of the ground—thinks it's still hot, and I don't blame him. The fire has singed him pretty well as it is."

The Indians sat their mounts as motionless as statues, the ponies headed directly toward where the two lads were lying.

"I'll bet they're got guns under those blankets," decided Tad. "You can't trust an Indian even while you are looking at him."

"Anybody'd think you'd been hunting Indians all your life," growled Stacy.

"They've been hunting me mostly," grinned Tad.

"And usually caught you," added Chunky.

"I don't like this lying here as if we were scared of them."

"But, what else can we do, Tad?"

"I don't know."

"Neither do I. Wish I had a shirt. I'll spoil my complexion clear down to my waist. Besides, I'm not fit to be seen."

"You're lucky to be alive," growled Tad. "I'm going to get out of this."

"How?"

"Listen, and you'll know. I'm going to get on the pony; then, as soon as I'm in the saddle, you jump up behind me and we'll start back to camp."

"Not—not through that fire?" protested Stacy.

"No; I don't dare try it. I'm afraid we'd get lost in the smoke and perhaps get burned as well. We'll ride out some distance, then turn to the left and try to go around the burned district."

"What if the Indians chase us?"

"I don't believe they will. They'll hardly dare do that. And, besides, these may be friendly Indians."

"Huh!" grunted Stacy. "They look it."

Tad got up boldly, and without even looking toward the silent red men, began fussing about his saddle, cinching the girths, and straightening the saddle. His last act before mounting was to see that the coils of his lariat were in order.

"All right," announced the lad, vaulting into the saddle.

Stacy scrambled up behind him without loss of time, and they rode out into the open, the fat boy peering apprehensively over his companion's shoulder.

"You keep watch of them, Chunky, but don't let them see you doing it. I won't look at them at all. We don't want them to think we're afraid."

Stacy fidgeted.

"You bet I'll watch 'em. Wish I had my rifle."

"I don't."

"Huh!"

"You have distinguished yourself quite enough with that rifle as it is. We don't want any more of your fancy shooting."

"There they go," warned Stacy.

"I see them." Tad had been cautiously observing the horsemen out of the corners of his eyes. "Moving in the same direction we are. I don't like the looks of it. Still, if they don't get any nearer we may be thankful."

The pony carrying the boys was walking easily, and the mounts of the Indians were doing the same.

"Jog a little," suggested Stacy.

"That's a good idea. It will tell us quickly whether they are trying to keep up with us."

He touched the pony lightly with his spurs. The little animal switched its tail, for its sides were tender, and started off.

"There they go, Tad! Jogging the same gait as ours!"

Tad's face took on the stubborn look it always wore when he had determined upon a certain course of action.

"I'll beat them yet, even if there are only two of them. I wish there weren't two of us on this nag."

"I'll get off and walk," suggested. Stacy.

"You'll do nothing of the sort. That would be a nice thing to do, wouldn't it? They'd round you up quicker'n they could a lame burro."

"Say, Tad."

"What?"

"I've got an idea."

"What is it?"

"You know that sage hen we had?"

"Yes, what's that got to do with our present predicament?"

"I was wondering why there aren't any sage roosters?"

"You'll be a sage rooster, with your head off, first thing you know," snapped Tad in disgust. "Can't you be serious for a minute? Don't you see we are in a fix?"

"Uh-huh!"

"There, that fellow is trying to head us off."

One of the Indians had shot away from his companion, running obliquely toward the point to which Tad was headed.

The red man had gotten quite a start before the boys caught the significance of his manoeuvre.

Tad dug in the spurs.

At that instant the fat boy's hands had been removed from Tad, to whose body they had been clinging.

The pony leaped forward, and Stacy slid over its rump, hitting the ground with a jolt that jarred him.

"Wow!" howled Stacy.

Tad, instantly divining what had happened, pulled up sharply; wheeled and raced back to where his companion was still complaining loudly and rubbing his body.

"Get up!" roared Tad, leaning over and grasping Stacy by the hair of his head.

The fat boy was jerked sharply to his feet.

"Quick! Quick, climb up here!"

With the help of his companion, the lad scrambled up behind Tad again, muttering and rubbing himself.

By this time the leading horseman had wholly outdistanced them, and his pony was now loping along easily, while the second Indian appeared to be riding directly toward them, at right angles to the direction in which they were traveling.

All at once the two Indians began riding about the boys in a circle, uttering short little "yips," intended to terrify the lads, but not loud enough to be heard any great distance away.

"Hang on! We're going to ride for keeps now!" warned Tad.

The fat boy threw both arms about his companion's waist as the pony let out into a swift run. At first Tad thought he had gotten safely out of the circle, only to discover that they had headed him again.

The circle was narrowing, and the Indians were gradually drawing in on them.

Stacy's eyes were growing larger every minute, perhaps more from astonishment than from fear. Then, too, he could not but admire the riding of their pursuers. Even the blankets of the Indians appeared not to be disturbed in the least by their rapid riding, the horsemen sitting a little sideways on the ponies' backs, the reins bunched loosely in their left bands.

"They've got us, Tad."

"They shan't get us!" retorted Tad stubbornly. "If they don't use their guns—and I don't believe they will—we'll beat them yet."

If Stacy was doubtful he did not say so.

"If they get close to us, you be ready to let go of me when I give the word," cautioned Tad.

"What for? What you going to do?"

"I don't know yet. That depends upon circumstances. I'm not going to let them have it all their own way while I've got a pony under me. We may get help any minute, too, so the longer we can put off a clash the better it will be for us."

"Who you mean—Santa Claus?"

"Yes."

"They're closing in now," said Stacy.

"Take your hands away from my waist."

"But I'll fall off, Tad."

"Slip one hand through under my belt and take hold of the cantle with the other. Sit as low as you can so as not to get in my way."

Stacy obeyed his companion's directions without further comment, but he was all curiosity to know what was going to happen next.

The Indians were drawing nearer every second now. The boys could see the expressions on their evil faces, intensified by the streaks of yellow and red paint.

"They look as though they'd stuck their heads in a paint pail," was Chunky's muttered comment.

The blankets fell away from the racing savages, flapped on the rumps of the bobbing ponies for a few seconds and then slipped to the ground.

A rifle was reposing in each man's holster, as Tad observed instantly. He was thankful to note that the guns were not in the hands of the Indians.

The lad's right hand had dropped carelessly to the saddle horn, the fingers cautiously gathering in the coils of the lariat that hung there. The red men did not appear to have observed his act.

"Lie low!" commanded Tad, scarcely above a whisper.

Stacy settled down slowly so as not to attract attention.

One horseman shot directly across Tad's course, striking the lad's pony full in the face as he did so, and causing the animal to brace himself so suddenly as to nearly unseat both boys.

Tad's rope was in the air in a twinkling.

A warning shout from the second Indian, who was just to the rear of them, came too late. The rope shot true to its mark and the first savage, with back half-turned, had failed to observe it coming.

The great loop dropped over his head. The pony braced itself and Tad took a quick turn of the rope about the pommel of his saddle.

The result was instantaneous. The Indian was catapulted from his saddle with arms pinioned to his aide.

"Ye-ow!" howled Chunky; unable to restrain his enthusiasm.

Tad did not even hear him.

"Look out! Here comes the other one!" warned the fat boy.

But Tad was too busily engaged in keeping the line taut about the roped Indian. The fellow was struggling on the ground, fighting to free himself, while the boy with the rope was manoeuvring his pony in a series of lightning-like movements that made the fat boy's head swim.

"Take care of him, Chunky!! I can't," gasped Tad.

Stacy's eyes took on a belligerent expression as the second savage bore down upon them, with knees gripped tightly against the side of his pony, half raising himself above the animal's back, reins dropped on the pony's neck. The Indian was guiding his mount by the pressure of legs and knees alone.

The angry redskin was making futile attempts to get into a position where he might grab the active Tad. He did not seem to take into account the cringing figure behind the boy who had roped the other Indian.

All at once, at the opportune moment, his pony forging ahead, the Indian's hand shot out. The red, bony fingers were closing upon Tad Butler's right shoulder, when all at once something happened.

The cringing fat boy rose. The right hand that had been clinging to the cantle was launched out. His body, thrown forward at the same time, lent the blow added force.

Chunky's fist came into violent contact with the Indian's jaw. Mr. Redman disappeared from the back of his pony so quickly that, for a second, Stacy could scarcely believe his eyes.

"Y-e-o-w! W-o-w!" howled the fat boy. "Beat it for the tall grass, Tad!"

A quick glance behind him, revealed the true state of affairs to Tad Butler. He dug in the spurs, clinging to the lariat for a few feet, then suddenly releasing it, as the pony leaped away under the stinging pressure of the spurs.

"Duck! Duck! They're going to shoot!" shouted Tad.

CHAPTER XV.
HIT BY A DRY STORM

"There it goes! Lower, Chunky!"

A rifle had crashed somewhere to the left of them.

Stacy's curiosity getting the better of him, he had twisted his body around, and was peering back; but he was bobbing up and down so fast that he found it difficult to fix his eyes on any one point long enough to distinguish what that object was.

"Look! Look!" he cried, when in a long rise of the pony his eyes had caught something definite.

The roped Indian was running for his pony, which he caught, leaping to its back and dashing away madly.

"Hold up! Hold up! There's something doing," shouted the fat, boy.

Tad swerved a little, turning to his left. Rifles were banging, and the dust was spurting up under the feet of the savage's racing pony.

By this time, the second Indian had recovered from the blow that Stacy had landed on his jaw, and he too was in his saddle in a twinkling, tearing madly cross the plain.

Stacy Brown uttered a series of wild whoops and yells. He knew their assailants were running and that some one was shooting at the Indians, but who it was the fat boy could only guess.

Two ponies suddenly dashed out from the low-lying smoke cloud. One of their riders was swinging his sombrero and cheering; the other was firing his rifle after the fleeing savages.

"Hooray, it's Santa Claus," howled Stacy, fairly beside himself with excitement. Even Tad caught something of his companion's spirit of enthusiasm. He swung his hand and started galloping toward the two horsemen.

"Shoot 'em! Kill 'em!" howled Chunky.

But Santa Claus merely shook his head, and after refilling the magazine of his rifle slipped it into the holster.

"It would only make trouble and probably cause an uprising if I did. They know I could have winged them both had I wanted to," he grinned. "Well, you boys are a sight."

"I—I lost my shirt," interjected Stacy.

"And I suppose you fell in," chuckled Ned.

"No; I fell off."

"We're lucky to be alive," laughed Tad.

"You are that. I see now that Professor Zepplin was right when he said you could take care of yourself. Never saw anything quite so slick as the way you roped that redskin—"

"And—and I punched the other one," glowed Chunky.

"Did you see us?" questioned Tad.

"Yes, we saw the whole proceeding. But you were so mixed up that we couldn't fire without danger of hitting one of you boys. Wonder what those Apaches think struck them," laughed the guide. "How did you get through the fire?"

Tad explained briefly; at the same time accounting for the loss of Stacy's shirt.

"I bet that the fellow with the canary-wing face has a sore jaw," bubbled Stacy.

"No doubt of it, Master Stacy. I didn't suppose you had such a punch as that. You're a good Indian fighter."

"Always was," answered the fat boy, swelling with importance.

"Come, we'll have to hurry back It will be dark before we reach camp, as it is, and the Professor will be worrying about you."

They turned about, and, heading across the burned area, started for camp. Fitful blazes were springing up here and there, but all danger had, by this time, passed, though the smoke still hung heavy and the odor of burned vegetation smote the nostrils unpleasantly.

Stacy sniffed the air suspiciously.

"Tastes like a drug store fire I smelled once in Chillicothe," he averred.

"I haven't made up my mind, yet, how that fire started, Mr. Kringle," wondered Tad.

"I have," replied the guide tersely.

"How?"

"It was set afire!"

"By whom?"

"By one of those savages, or by somebody who was with them. They must have been watching you all the time. Did you recognize either of them as the fellow you knocked down the other might?"

"No; I don't think I would know the Indian. The light was too uncertain at the fire dance, and then again, all Indians look alike to me."

"It was a narrow escape."

"Do you think they'll come back again?" questioned Ned.

"I doubt it. They won't if they recognized me. They know me. They've done business with me before."

Professor Zepplin and Walter were overjoyed when at last the party rode into camp and they learned that both boys were safe. The lads were obliged to go all over their experiences again for the benefit of the Professor and Walter.

"It's getting worse and worse," decided the Professor helplessly. "I don't know where all this is going to end. I thought when we got a new guide—but what's the use? Do you think we had better start to-night, Mr. Kringle?"

"No. There is no necessity."

"What am I going to do for a pony?" asked Chunky.

"You can ride one of mine. I always take two when on a long journey," replied the guide.

Chunky's first act after reaching camp, was to provide himself with a shirt. After donning it, he announced that he had an appetite and wanted to know when they were going to have supper.

"Why, you had supper hours ago," scoffed Ned. "Want another one already?"

"That wasn't supper, that was four o'clock tea. Indian fighters must have real food."

"Stop teasing. We'll give the 'ittle baby his milk," returned Ned.

That night, Kris Kringle remained on guard himself. He would not trust the guardianship of the camp to any of the boys, for he fully expected that they would receive a visit from one or more of the Indians, though he did not tell the others so. But nothing occurred to disturb the camp, and the boys, despite their trying experiences, slept soundly, awakening in the morning fresh and active, ready and anxious for any further adventures.

The party set out shortly after sunrise, and traveled all day across the uneven plains, across short mountain ranges, through deep gorges and rugged foothills.

Crossing an open space the guide espied a bottle glistening in the sunlight.

"There's a bottle," pointed the guide. "Want it?"

Stacy glanced at it indifferently;

"What do I want of a bottle?"

"Then I'll take it," decided the guide, dismounting and stowing the abandoned piece of glass in his saddle bags.

"Bottles are good for only two things."

"And what are they, Master Stacy?" questioned the Professor.

"To keep things in and to shoot at," replied the fat boy wisely.

Everybody laughed at that.

"I guess that embodies everything you can say about bottles," smiled the Professor. "Your logic, at times, young man, is unassailable."

Chunky nodded. He had a faint idea of what Professor Zepplin meant.

Late that afternoon the travelers came upon a shack in the foothills, where an old rancher, a hermit, lived when not tending his little flock of sheep, most of which, Kris Kringle said, the old man had stolen from droves that came up over the trail going north.

He was an interesting old character, this hermit, and the boys decided that they would like to make camp and have him take supper with them. This the Professor and the guide readily agreed to, for everyone was hot and dusty and the bronchos were nervous and ill-natured.

The boys found the old rancher talkative enough on all subjects save himself. When Chunky asked him where he came from, and what for, the old man's face flushed angrily.

At the first opportunity the guide took the fat boy aside for some fatherly advice.

"In this country it isn't good policy to be too curious about a man's family affairs. He's likely to resent it in a way you won't like. Most fellows out here have reasons for being out of the world, beyond what's apparent on the surface."

Chunky heeded the advice and asked no more personal questions for the next hour, though he did forget himself before the evening was ended.

"You seem to be having pretty dry weather down here," said the Professor, by way of starting the old man to talking.

"Yep. Haven't had any rain in this belt fer the last two years."

"Two years!" exclaimed the boys.

"Yep. Had a few light dews, but that's all," replied the hermit.

"Looks to me as if you were going to get some to-night," announced Tad.

"Reckon not."

"Then I'm no judge of weather."

Even as Tad spoke there was a low muttering of thunder, and the far lightning flashed pale and green, and rose on the long horizon to the southwest.

Kris Kringle heard the far away growl. Springing up, he began staking down the tents.

"That's a good idea. We lost our whole outfit on our last trip. Think they'll stand a blow?"

"I guess they will when I get through with them. Have we any more stakes in camp?"

"There should be some in the kit."

Tad searched until he found several more stakes, and with these and the emergency ropes, they made the tents secure.

By the time they had done so, the heavens had grown black and menacing. They could see the storm sweeping down on them. It was a magnificent sight, and the lads were so lost in observing its grandeur that they forgot to feel any alarm.

A cloud of dust accompanied the advance guard of the storm.

"Reckon there ain't any rain in them clouds," commented the old man. "There's plenty of the other thing, though."

"What's the other thing?" questioned Chunky.

"Lightning."

Even as he spoke a bolt descended right in the center of the camp, tearing a hole in the earth and hurling a cloud of dirt and dust many feet up into the air.

The force of the explosion knocked some of the party flat.

Chunky picked himself up and carefully brushed his clothes; then, solemnly walked out and sat down on the spot where the lightning had struck.

"Here, here! What are you doing out there?" demanded the guide.

"Sitting on the lightning."

"You come in here! And quick, at that!"

"Huh! Guess I know what I'm doing. Lightning never strikes twice in the same place. I'm—"

By this time Kris Kringle had the fat boy by the collar, hustling him to the protection of one of the tents.

No sooner had they reached it than a crash that seemed as if it had split the earth wide open descended upon them. Balls of fire shot off in every direction. One went right through the tent where they were huddled, hurling the Pony Rider Boys in a heap.

They scrambled up calling to each other nervously.

The shock had extinguished the lantern that hung in the tent. The guide relighted it, and, stepping outside to see what had happened, pointed to the place where Chunky had been sitting but a few minutes before.

The bolt had struck in the identical spot where the previous one had landed.

"Now, young man, there's an object lesson for you," Mr. Kringle said, with a grim smile.

"And there's another!" replied Chunky, pointing to the outside of the tent.

There lay the old rancher, whose absence they had not noted. He had been in the tent with them when they last saw him and how he had gotten out there none knew. The rancher had been stripped of every vestige of clothing by the freaky lightning.

"He's dead," crooned Stacy solemnly.

"Get water, quick! He's been struck by lightning!" commanded the guide, making systematic efforts to bring the old man back to consciousness.

Stacy ran for the water-bags.

"I am afraid it is useless, Mr. Kringle," warned, the Professor, failing to find a pulse. The boys were standing about fanning the victim, having one by one dumped the contents of their canteens in his face.

Stacy returned with a water-bag after a little.

"I—I—I've got an idea," he exploded, as with eyes wide open he attempted to tell them something.

"Keep still. We've got something else to do besides listening to your foolishness," chided Ned.

"Chunky, we're trying to save this man's life. Give me that bag," commanded Tad.

The two older men were working desperately on the patient. Stacy stood around, fidgeting a little, but making no further attempt to enlighten them as to what his new idea was.

After a time the rancher began to show signs of recovering. He gasped a few times then opened his eyes.

"What kicked me?" he asked, with a half-grin.

They could all afford to laugh now, and they did. The rancher refused their offer of clothes, saying he had another suit in his shack.

"That's twice the stuff has knocked me out. Next time it'll git me for keeps," he said.

"Does it strike here very often?" questioned the Professor.

"Allus."

"Then, there must be some mineral substance in the soil."

"No, ain't nothing like that. Jest contrariness that's all. Hit my shack once, and 'cause 'twas raining, bored holes in the roof so the place got all wet inside."

"But it isn't raining now. Doesn't it usually rain when you have a thunder storm here?" asked the Professor.

"No. Ain't had no rain in nigh onto two year," the hermit reiterated.

"You'd better go and put on some clothes," suggested Kris Kringle.

"Guess that's right."

The old man seemed to have forgotten his condition. The others had wrapped a blanket around him, which seemed to satisfy his demand for clothes. Gathering up the blanket he strolled leisurely toward his cabin, undisturbed by his recent experience.

"Nothing like getting used to it," chuckled Stacy.

"Hello, now we'll hear what your new idea is, Chunky?" jeered Ned.

"Yes, what is it?" urged Tad.

"Nothing much."

"Never is," cut in Walter Perkins, a little maliciously.

"I—I got an idea the ponies tried to kick holes in the lightning."

Everybody laughed loudly. They could well afford to laugh, now that the danger had passed.

"What makes you think that?" asked the guide, eyeing him sharply.

"'Cause they're dead!"

"What!" shouted the boys.

All hands dashed from the tent, Stacy regarding them with soulful eyes, after which he surreptitiously slipped a biscuit into his pocket and strolled out after them.

CHAPTER XVI.
CHUNKY'S NEW IDEA

Three of the ponies, they found, had been knocked down and so severely shocked that they were only just beginning to regain consciousness.

"Why didn't you tell us?" demanded Ned, turning on Stacy savagely.

"You wouldn't let me. Maybe next time I've got an idea, you'll stop and listen."

Kris Kringle's face wore a broad grin.

"Master Stacy is right. He tried hard enough to tell us," he said.

Chunky was humming blithely as the party set out next morning. He was pretty well satisfied with himself, for had he not been through a prairie fire, knocked a savage Apache off his horse, saved himself and his companions, besides having just escaped from being struck by lightning? Stacy swelled out his chest and held his chin a little bit higher than usual.

"Chunky's got a swelled head," said Ned, nodding in the direction of the fat boy.

"Swelled chest, you mean," laughed Walter. "Nobody has a better right. Chunky isn't half as big a fool as he'd have everybody believe. When we think we are having lots of fun with him he's really having sport with us. And those Indians— say, Ned, do you think they will bother us any more?"

"Ask Chunky," retorted Ned. "He's the oracle of the party."

"I will," answered Walter, motioning for Stacy to join them, which the latter did leisurely. "We want to know if you think we've seen the last of the Apaches? Will they bother us any more?"

The fat boy consulted the sky thoughtfully.

"I think there's some of them around now," he replied.

"What?"

Stacy nodded wisely.

"Santa Claus ought to have shot them."

"Why, you cold-blooded savage!" scoffed Ned. "The idea!"

"You'll see. I'd have done it, myself, if I'd had my gun," declared Stacy bravely.

"Good thing for you that your gun was in camp, instead of in your holster."

"Yes; I'd have lost the gun when the pony went down. Poor pony! Say, Walt," he murmured, leaning over toward his companion.

"Well, out with it!"

"This pony of Santa Claus's can jump further than a kangaroo."

"Ever see a kangaroo jump?" sneered Ned.

"No; but I've seen you try to. I'll show you, Walt, when we get a chance to go out and have a contest."

"That would be good sport, wouldn't it, Ned?"

"What?"

"A jumping contest!"

"If we didn't break our necks."

"Can't break a Pony Rider Boy's neck. They're too tough," laughed Walter, to which sentiment, Stacy Brown agreed with a series of emphatic nods.

"Say, Tad," called Walter, "what do you say to our jumping our ponies some time to-day?"

Tad grinned appreciatively.

"If the stock isn't too tired when we make camp, I think it would be great fun. We haven't had any real jumping contests in a long time."

"Wish we had our stallions here, Tad."

"They're better off at home, Chunky. Altogether too valuable horses for this kind of work. I'll speak to the guide."

"Well, what is it, young man?" smiled Kris Kringle.

"If you can find a level place for our camp we want to have a contest this afternoon. Professor, will you join us?"

"What kind of a contest?"

"Jumping."

"No, thank you."

"We will camp in the foothills of the Black range. You will find plenty of level ground there for your purpose," said the guide.

In order that they might have more time for their games, an early halt was called. The first work was to pitch the camp, the ponies being allowed to graze and rest in the meantime, after which the lads started out on a broad, open plain for their sport.

Their shouts of merriment drifted back to the camp where Kris Kringle and Professor Zepplin were setting things to rights and preparing an early supper, the sun still being some hours high.

"That's a great bunch of boys, Professor."

"Great for getting into difficulties."

"And for getting out of them."

"I'll put them against any other four lads in the world for hunting out trouble," laughed the Professor.

The result of the afternoon's sport was a total of several spills and numerous black and blue spots on the bodies of the Pony Rider Boys. Stacy Brown on Kris Kringle's pony, carried off the honors, having taken a higher jump than did any of his companions. Then Stacy did it again, after the others had tried—and failed to equal the record.

The games being finished, Tad and Walter rode off to get a closer view of some peculiar rock formations that they had discovered in the high distance, while Ned and Chunky started slowly for the camp.

The table had been set out in front of the tents when the fat boy and his companion came in sight of the camp.

"Whew! but I'm hungry!" announced Stacy Brown.

"But you didn't think of it until you saw the table set, did you?"

"It wasn't the table, it was the shaking up I got back there that made me feel full of emptiness."

"Huh!"

"I've got an idea, Ned."

"For goodness' sake, keep it to yourself, then. When you have an idea it spells trouble for everybody else around you."

"Bet you I can."

"Can what?" snorted Ned.

"Bet you I can jump the dinner table and you can't."

"Bet you can't."

"Bet I can, and without even knocking a fly off the milk pitcher."

"Go on, you! You try it first, and, if you don't make it, you lose. I don't have to try it if I don't want to," agreed Ned, with rare prudence.

Chunky was fairly hugging himself with glee, but he took good care that Ned Rector did not observe his satisfaction.

"If you don't you're a tenderfoot," taunted Stacy.

"I'll show you who's the tenderfoot. You go ahead and bolt the dinner, table and all, if you dare. Now, then!"

Stacy gathered up his reins. There was mischief in his eyes, which were fixed on the table, neatly set for the evening meal.

"You start right after me. They'll be surprised to see a procession of ponies going over the table, won't they?"

"Somebody'll be surprised. May not be the Professor and Santa Claus, though," growled Ned.

Stacy had his own ideas on this question, but he did not confide them to his companion.

The fat boy clucked to his pony, and the little animal started off. As they moved along, Stacy used the persuasive spurs resulting in a sudden burst of speed.

"Come on!" he shouted.

He heard Ned's pony pursuing him.

"Hi-yi-yi-y-e-o-w!" howled the shrill voice of the fat boy.

Professor Zepplin and Kris Kringle were sitting at opposite ends of the table, with elbows leaning on it, engaged in earnest conversation. There had been so much yelling out on the plain ever since the boys left camp that the older men gave no heed to this new shout—did not even turn their eyes in the direction whence Stacy Brown and his pony were sweeping down on them at break-neck speed.

Suddenly the two men started back with a sudden exclamation, as a shadow fell athwart the table and a dark form hurled itself through the air, while a shrill, "w-h-o-o-p-e-e!" sounded right over their heads.

The fat boy cleared the table without so much as disturbing the fly to which he had referred when making the arrangement.

Kris Kringle's face wore an expansive grin as he discovered the cause of the interruption. But, Professor Zepplin's face reflected no such emotion. He was angry. He started to rise, when a second shadow fell across the table.

Ned Rector, not to be outdone by his fat little friend, pursed his lips tightly, driving his broncho at the dinner table and pressing in the spurs so hard, that the pony grunted with anger.

Up went the broncho in a graceful curving leap.

But the pony or its rider had not calculated the distance properly. Both rear hoofs went through the table, whisking it off the ground from before the astonished eyes of Professor Zepplin and Kris Kringle.

Both men drew back so violently that they toppled over backwards.

'Mid the crashing of dishes and the sound of breaking wood, the dinner table shot up into the air, while the pony ploughed the ground with its nose.

Ned Rector struck the ground some distance farther on; he slid on his face for several feet skinning his nose, and filling mouth, eyes and nose with dirt.

Then dishes and pieces of table began to rain down on them in a perfect shower. A can of condensed milk emptied itself on the head of Professor Zepplin, while a hot biscuit lodged inside the collar of Santa Claus's shirt.

"Wow! Oh, wow!" howled the fat boy, falling off his pony in the excess of his merriment and rolling on the ground.

CHAPTER XVII.
IN THE HOME OF THE CAVE DWELLERS

Ned Rector sat up just in time to meet the wreck of the descending table. Down he went again with Stacy's howls ringing in his ears.

A firm hand jerked Rector free of the debris as Kris Kringle laughing heartily hauled Ned to his feet. At the same moment Professor Zepplin had laid more violent hands on the fat boy, whom he shook until Stacy's howls lost much of their mirth. About this time Tad and Walter rode in, having hurried along upon hearing the disturbance in camp.

"Stacy Brown, are you responsible for this?" demanded the Professor sternly.

"I'm more to blame than he is," interposed Ned.

"No, I—I had an idea," chuckled Stacy, threatening to break out into another howl of mirth.

"Next time you have one, then, you will be good enough to let me know. We will tie you up until the impulse to make trouble has passed."

Tad and Walter could not resist a shout of laughter. Kris Kringle was not slow to follow the example set by them, and all at once Professor Zepplin forgot his dignity, sitting right down amid the wreck and laughing immoderately.

Ned washed his face, and when, upon facing them, he exhibited a peeled nose and a black eye, the merriment was renewed again.

Supper was a success, in spite of the fact that many of their dishes were utterly ruined, as well as some of the provisions. But the lads gathered up the pieces and made the best of a bad job. Fortunately they carried another folding table that they had had made for their trip, and this was soon spread and a fresh meal prepared.

"Well, have you two been getting into difficulties also?" questioned the Professor, after they sat down to supper.

"No; we've been exploring, Walter and I," answered Tad.

"Exploring?"

"Yes. We discovered something that I should like to know more about."

"What is that?" asked Kris Kringle, looking up interestedly.

"We were over yonder, close to the mountains, which are straight up and down, and half way to the top, we saw three or four queerly-shaped rocks that looked like houses or huts. Did you ever see them, Mr. Kringle?"

"No; but I think I know what you mean. They must be some of the cave dwellings of the ancient Pueblos, or perhaps as far back as the Toltecs. They built their homes in caves on the steep rocks for better protection against their enemies."

"And nobody ever discovered these before?" questioned. Walter. "How queer!"

"Perhaps these dwellings, if such they are, have been seen by many a traveler, none of whom had interest enough in the matter to investigate. Then again, they may have been fully explored. There's not much in this part of the country that prospectors have not looked over."

"May we explore these caves, Professor?" asked Tad.

"Please let us?" urged Walter.

"I see no objection if Mr. Kringle will be responsible for you. I rather think I'll look into them myself. I'll confess the idea interests me. Are they easy to get at?"

"I'm afraid not," answered Tad.

"Santa Claus will show us the way," interrupted Stacy enthusiastically.

He was frowned down by the Professor.

"Why not start now?" urged Tad.

The guide consulted the sun.

"We might. It lacks all of three hours to dark."

There was much enthusiasm in camp. The idea that they were to visit some unexplored caves, dwellings of an ancient people, filled the lads with pleasant expectancy.

Before starting, Mr. Kringle sorted out some strong manila rope and several tent stakes all of which he did up into two bundles. Then he filled the magazine of his rifle, throwing this over his shoulder.

"What's that for?" questioned Ned.

"The gun?"

"Yes."

"Can't tell what we may run into in a cave, you know."

After a final look at the camp all hands set out for the place indicated by Tad. It was only a short distance, so they decided to walk.

Reaching the base of the mountain they gazed up.

"Yes, those are cave dwellings," declared Kris Kringle. "And they are still closed. Probably they haven't been opened in two hundred years."

"I'd hate to live there and have to go home in a dark night," mused Chunky.

"Yes, how did they get to their houses?" wondered the other boys.

"The question is, how are we going to get near enough to explore them? How shall we get up there, Mr. Guide?" asked the Professor.

"We'll find a way. We shall have to climb the mountain, first."

All hands began clambering up the rocks. To do so they were obliged to follow along the base of the mountain for some distance before they found a place that they could climb.

Reaching the top, the guide examined their surroundings carefully.

"See those little projections of rock slanting down toward the shelf?" he asked.

"Yes."

"Well, in the old days they probably felled a tree so it would fall on them. The occupants of the cave probably cut steps in the tree trunk over which to travel up and down. The tree has rotted away many years since."

"And we can't get down, then?"

"We'll find a way, Master Walter. I thought I should be able to make a rope ladder that would work, but I see it is not practicable."

"How shall we do it?"

"Try the old way, I guess, Master Tad."

"What's that?"

"The tree."

"But there are no trees near here?"

"Yes, there are, a few rods back. We are all strong and I guess we shall be able to make a pretty fair pair of steps."

Kris Kringle had brought an axe with him. With this he cut some long, straight poles which, he explained, were intended for pike poles such as woodsmen use to roll logs. This done, he began industriously chopping at the tree after deciding upon the exact position in which he desired it to fall.

"It won't reach," declared Chunky, who, with hands in pockets, legs spread wide apart, stood looking up at the flaring top of the great tree.

The guide stopped chopping long enough to squint at the fat boy.

"It'll reach you all right, if you stay where you are," he said, then resumed his vigorous blows.

Stacy promptly took the hint and moved a safe distance away.

"Get from under!" shouted the guide finally. One more blow would send the tree crashing downward.

All hands scrambled for safety. One powerful blow from the axe, and with a crashing and rending, the great tree began its descent. When it struck the onlookers fully expected to see it broken into many pieces, but the bushy top, hitting the rocks first, broke the blow, and the body of the tree settled down gently without even breaking its bark.

"Fine! Hurrah!" shouted the boys.

"It won't reach to the edge. Going to pull it over?" questioned Stacy.

"Not exactly, but we're going to get it there. Perhaps we shall not have it in place in time to explore the caves to-night, but we shall be ready to do so early in the morning. It took our friends longer to do this job, two hundred years or more ago, than it will take us. We have better tools to work with."

"And better bosses," suggested Stacy.

Some little time was consumed in chopping the tree loose from its stump, after which the guide worked the pike poles under the trunk at intervals near the base. The others watched these operations with interest.

"Now here is where you young gentlemen will have a chance to show how strong you are. Each one grab a pike pole," Kringle directed.

"Shan't I go hold the top down?" asked Stacy.

"You just grab a pike pole and get busy!" laughed Mr. Kringle.

"Can't get out of work quite so easy as you thought," scoffed Ned. "This is where we make you earn your supper."

"I don't have to earn it. Had it already."

"There are other meals coming," smiled the Professor.

"Now, heo—he!"

All raised on the pike poles at the same time with the result that the tree was forced down the gentle incline several feet. This was repeated again and again, the boys pausing to cheer after every lift.

The tree being now perilously near the edge of the cliff Kris Kringle called a halt. Next he fastened a rope around the top and another around the base, taking a turn around a rock with each. One boy was placed on each rope, the others at the pike poles, while the guide stood at the edge giving directions.

The tree trunk gently slipped over under his guidance and a few minutes later rested on the projecting rocks, that were just high enough to hold it in place.

"Wouldn't take much to send it over, but I guess it will be perfectly safe," he mused.

"May we go down now?" cried the boys.

"No; I'll make some steps first."

He did so with the axe, chopping out scoop-shaped places for steps, until finally he had reached the rock in front of the cave dwellings.

The tree lay at an easy slope, its bushy top partly resting on the ledge, the latter being some eight feet deep by ten feet wide.

Running up the log Mr. Kringle made another rope fast at the top, throwing the free end over.

"Hold on to the rope while you are going down and you'll be in no danger of falling," he warned.

The boys scrambled down the tree like so many squirrels, the Professor following somewhat more cautiously.

The explorers found themselves not more than twenty feet from the ground.

"Not much of a door yard. Where's the garden?" wondered Stacy, looking about him curiously.

The entrance to the cave dwelling was blocked by a huge boulder, that completely filled the opening. How it had been gotten there none could say. The only possible explanation was that the boulder had been found on the shelf and applied to the purpose of protecting the cave dwellers' home.

"Now we're here, we can't get in," grumbled Ned.

"Nothing is impossible," answered Kris Kringle.

"Except one thing."

"What's that, Master Ned?"

"To hammer the least little bit of sense into the head of my friend, Chunky Brown."

"You don't have to, that's why," retorted Stacy quickly. "It has all the sense it'll hold, now."

"I guess that will be about all for you, Ned," laughed Walter. "At least, Chunky didn't foul the dinner table when he jumped it."

The guide, in the meantime, was experimenting with the boulder, inserting a pike pole here and there in an effort to move the big stone. It remained in place as solidly as if it had grown there.

"There's some trick about the thing, I know, but what it is gets me. Better stand back, all of you, in case it comes out all of a sudden," Mr. Kringle warned them.

All at once the boulder did come out, and it kept on coming.

"Look out!" bellowed the guide.

"Low bridge!" howled Stacy, hopping to one side and crouching against the rocks.

The guide had sprung nimbly to one side as well. The big rock had popped out like a pea from a pod. Instead of stopping, however, it continued to roll on toward the edge.

"Hug the rocks! She's going down!" shouted the guide.

Go down it did, with a crash that seemed to shake the mountain. Rolling to the edge of the shelf, it had toppled over, taking a large strip of shelving rock with it.

"Wow!" howled Chunky;

The other boys uttered no sound, though their faces were a little more pale than usual.

Kris Kringle stepped to the edge, peering over.

"No one will get that up here again, right away," he said.

"The cave, the cave!" shouted Walter.

Everyone turned, gazing half in awe at the dark opening that the removal of the stone had revealed—an opening that had been closed for probably more than two centuries.

CHAPTER XVIII.
FACING THE ENEMY'S GUNS

"Do we go in?" asked the Professor.

"Wait, I'll get some light inside first," answered the prudent guide. "Can't tell whether we shall want to go in or not."

He built up a small fire within, then called to the others that they might enter. They crowded in hastily, finding themselves in a fairly large chamber, at the far end of which was a sort of natural alcove in the rocks.

The remnants of a fire still lay at one side, where the last meal of the ancient dweller had probably been cooked. Several crude looking utensils lay about, together with a number of pieces of ancient pottery.

"This is, indeed, a rare find!" exclaimed the Professor, carrying the precious jars out into the light for closer examination.

Chunky, about that time, pounced upon an object which proved to be a copper hatchet.

"Hurray for George Washington!" he shouted, brandishing the crude tool. "The man who never told—"

"We've heard that before," objected Ned. "Give us something new, Chunky, if you've *got* to talk."

The Professor came in, searching for other curios just as Stacy went out to examine his "little axe," as he was pleased to call it. He tried the edge of it on the ledge to find out if the stone would dull it, but it did not.

"I'll use that to cut nails and wire with when I get back home," decided the boy. "Guess I'll chop my name in the side of the mountain here." Stacy proceeded to do so, the others being too much engrossed in their explorations to know or care what he was about. He succeeded very well, both in making letters on the wall and in putting several nicks in the edge of his new-found hatchet.

He was thus engaged when all at once something struck the axe hurling it from his hand. At the same instant a rifle crashed off somewhere below and to the southeast of him.

"Ouch!" exclaimed the fat boy holding his hand. "Wonder who did that?" His mind had not coupled the shot with the blow on the hatchet.

Bang!

A bullet flattened itself close to his head, against the rock.

With a howl, the lad threw himself down on the ledge.

At that instant Kris Kringle sprang to the opening of the cave.

"What does this mean?" he snapped.

"I don't know. Somebody knocked the axe out of my hand then shot at me."

The guide discovered the trouble right there. A bullet snipped his hat from his head; and, striking the ceiling of the cave-home, dropped to the floor with a dull clatter.

Kris Kringle ducked with amazing quickness. Crawling back into the cave, he reached for his own rifle and then sought the opening, taking good care not to expose himself to the fire of the unseen enemy.

Stacy, on his part, had lost no time in getting to a place of safety inside, though he was prudent enough to crawl instead of getting up and walking in.

"What does this mean? It can't be possible that anyone is deliberately shooting at us?" questioned Professor Zepplin in undisguised amazement.

"If you doubt it step outside," suggested Kris Kringle. "Master Stacy and myself know what they tried to do, don't we, lad?"

"We do."

The fat boy again swelled with importance.

"Look out you don't swell up so big you'll break your harness," warned Ned.

"Better break it than have it shot off," mumbled Stacy.

"Who can it be?"

"I can't say, Professor."

"It's our friends from the fire dance," was Tad's expressed conviction.

"Told you they'd be here," nodded Chunky. "Why don't you shoot at them?"

"Going to, in a minute. Got to find out where they are first."

Now the lads were excited in earnest. Some one was shooting at them, and the guide was going to fire back. This was more than they had expected when they visited the home of the cave-dweller.

"Let me take a crack at 'em," begged Chunky. "I owe 'em one."

"Master Stacy, you will do nothing of the sort," reproved the Professor sternly. "The idea!"

"No; if there's any shooting to be done I'll do it," announced Kris Kringle.

"And Santa Claus isn't shooting with any toy gun, this time," chuckled Chunky.

"Can you see the camp, to know if anyone is there?"

"Yes, but only part of it, Professor. I wish you would all get over into the right hand corner there and lie flat on the floor. I'm going to try to draw their fire so that I can locate them. Can't afford to waste ammunition until we are reasonably sure where our mark is."

The others quickly got into the position indicated.

Placing his hat on one of the pike poles, Kringle slowly pushed it outside.

There was no result, The ruse failed to draw the enemy's fire.

"Oh, they've gone. We're a lot of babies," jeered Ned, jumping up and starting for the opening.

Kris Kringle gave him a push with the butt of the rifle.

"Want, to get shot full of holes? Wait! I'll show you."

The guide sprang up, showing himself out on the ledge for one brief instant then throwing himself flat.

A sharp "ping" against the rocks, followed by a heavy report, told the story. The guide had been not a second too soon in getting out of harm's way, for the bullet would have gone right through him had he remained standing.

Quick as a flash Kringle's rifle leaped to his shoulder, and he fired. He had taken quick aim at a puff of smoke off toward the camp.

Not content with one shot he raked the bushes all about where the puff of smoke had been seen, emptying the magazine of the rifle in a few seconds.

Stacy Brown was fairly dancing with glee.

"Did you hit anything?" asked the boys breathlessly.

"Of course, I hit something; but whether I winged an Indian or not, I don't know. If I did, he probably is not seriously wounded. You'll hear a redskin yell when he's hit bad."

"That one I punched didn't. He was hit hard," volunteered Stacy.

"He didn't have time," grinned Tad. "You were too quick for him."

"Look out! There comes a volley!" warned Mr. Kringle.

The boys, led by the Professor tumbled into the corner in a heap, while the lead pattered in through the opening, rattling with great force like a handful of pebbles.

"They're getting in a hurry," averred the Professor.

"It's growing dark. They want to finish us before then, so we can't play any tricks on them after that. But, if they only knew it, and they probably do, they've got us beautifully trapped. One man below and another at the other end of our tree would be able to keep us here till the springs run dry. If there's only two of them there, as I suspect is the case, they may not want to separate. We'll see, the minute it gets dark enough so that we can move about without being observed."

Some of the sage brush that Kris Kringle had brought down to light up the cave lay outside on the ledge. Using one of the poles, he cautiously raked the stuff inside, heaping it up not far from the entrance.

"What you doing that for?" questioned Stacy, unable to conceal his curiosity.

"You'll see, by-and-by, when we get ready to do something else. You don't think I'm going to stay here all night, do you?"

There was no further firing on either side, though Mr. Kringle showed himself boldly several times.

Finally Tad tried it, and was greeted with a shot the instant he appeared in the opening.

"Must be me they're after," he suggested, with a forced grin, falling flat on the ledge, and wriggling back into the cave.

The twilight was upon them now. The guide had been able to see the flash of the rifle below him, and had taken a quick shot at it when the enemy attempted to wing Tad Butler. Kringle had no means of knowing whether his shot had been effective or not.

"I'm going to try something else in a few minutes, now," the guide told the Professor and the boys, "and I hope you all will do just as I tell you."

"You may depend upon our doing exactly that," answered the Professor.

"I am going to crawl out of here. The rest of you remain here until I call to you to come out, no matter if it is until morning. After I have been gone about ten minutes, light a match and toss it into the heap of sage there, but watch out that you don't get into the light. Throw the match. You're liable to be shot if you show yourselves."

"Why should we make a fire and thus make targets of ourselves?" protested Ned.

"That is to cover Mr. Kringle's retreat," Tad informed them.

"Exactly. Master Tad, you may come along with me if you wish."

Tad jumped at the offer.

"But not a sound. Ask me no questions. Follow a rod or so behind me, and walk low down all the time. If you make a mistake it may result seriously for you and your friends. And, another thing."

"Yes?"

"Should there be any shooting, throw yourself on the ground. You will not be as likely to be hit there."

"I'll obey orders, sir."

"I know it."

"When do we start?"

"I guess we can do so now, as safely as at any time. The rascals will not be likely to be on the mountain just yet, because it is not dark enough. Yes; we'll go now."

Tad waited until Kris Kringle had crawled from the cave, then lay down on his stomach and wriggled out on the ledge.

There were no signs of the enemy and the camp-fire of the Pony Rider Boys glowed dimly down below. Tad, peering off into the gloom, for the moon had not yet risen, thought he saw a figure flit by the fire. He could not be sure, however. He wished he might tell the guide of his fancied discovery; but, remembering the injunction for absolute silence, he said nothing.

By this time, Tad's arms were about the log. From the slight vibration he knew that Kris Kringle was somewhere between himself and the top, yet not a sound did the guide make. Tad made no more, and they would have been keen ears, indeed, that could have detected our friends' presence by sound alone.

When the lad finally reached the top a hand was laid on his shoulder. The touch gave him a violent start in spite of his steady nerves.

"You're all right," whispered the voice of Kris Kringle. "You'd make a good Indian. I want to explain something that I didn't wish the others to hear."

"Yes?" whispered Tad.

"I have only one shell left in my rifle. That's why I wanted you to go along. If, by any chance, the rascals should get me, you lie low. They'll make for the cave, as they know, by this time, that there is only one rifle in the party. The minute they do, should such an emergency arise, slide for the camp and get your gun. You'll know what to do with it. It'll be a case of saving the lives of your companions if it comes to that."

"I understand," answered Tad bravely; and without a quaver in his voice.

"Mind you, I don't think for a minute that it will happen. I can handle these fellows if I get the lay of the land. Keep close enough to hear me."

"That's not so easy."

"No; but you'll know. When I stop you do the same."

CHAPTER XIX.
OUTWITTING THE REDSKINS

Kris Kringle moved away without another word. His abrupt departure was the signal for the Pony Rider boy to start, which he did instantly.

In a few minutes Tad was skulking along the top of the mountain, when he ran into the guide again.

Just then the report of a rifle sounded down below them.

"Are they shooting at us?" whispered Tad.

"No; the boys have lighted the fire in the cave. Our friends down below took a pot shot at the blaze. Hope they didn't hit anybody."

"Chunky would be the only one to get in the way, and I imagine the others would hold him back."

"Come this way; we'll go down by a different trail. The redskins are watching the fire in the cave, but they may be keeping an eye on the trail at the same time."

Silently the man and the boy took their way along the rough, uneven path, slowly working down into the valley. They soon reached this, for the range was low there.

Reaching the foothills, the two scouts once more fell into single file, Tad Butler to the rear. He knew that the guide's rifle ahead of him was ready for instant use, and at any second now Tad expected to see the flash of a gun.

The lad was not afraid, but he was all a-quiver with excitement. This stalking an enemy in the dark, not knowing at what minute that enemy might make the attack, was not the same as a stand-up fight in broad daylight. Tad wondered why the guide had not permitted the rest of the party to escape while they had the opportunity. He did not know that Kris Kringle fully expected an ambush, nor that two would stand a better chance to get through and out-wit the savages than would half a dozen of them. The pair had approached nearly to the camp, for which the guide was heading, when suddenly a hand was laid on the boy's arm in a firm grip. Tad knew the guide had seen or heard something.

"What is it?"

"There!"

In the faint light of the camp-fire the lad, gazing where Kris Kringle had pointed, was astonished to see a figure seated at their table. From his motions it was evident that the intruder was stowing away the stolen fool at a great rate.

"Is that one of them?"

"Yes."

"He'll have indigestion, the way he's eating. Hope he doesn't swallow the dishes, too."

"I'm going to find the other one. You crawl as close to the camp as you can with safety. If you hear a disturbance, dive for the tents the instant that fellow starts. He'll move if he hears any noise. Get a gun and hurry to me, but be quiet about it."

"Yes."

"Remember your instructions. I may be able to handle both of them, but if I don't get the missing one at the first crack I shan't be able to take care of them both. You'll have to help me. Got the nerve?"

"I'm not afraid," whispered the boy steadily. "And I've got some muscle as well."

"That's evident. I'm off now."

Tad was left alone. This time he could feel the guide's movements, as the latter slipped away on the soft earth. But in a moment all sound was lost.

"I think I'll crawl up nearer, so as to be handy if anything occurs," decided the lad, creeping along on all fours. He could not see the light in the camp now, but he reasoned that the man at the table was sitting with his back to it, as near as Tad could judge of direction in the dark. The Indian seemed not to fear a surprise.

"That's what comes from overconfidence," grinned the lad.

"I wish I had something to defend myself with," he added after a pause.

Tad had no sooner expressed his wish, than his fingers closed over some object on the ground. He grasped it with about the same hopefulness that a dying man will grasp at a straw.

What he had found was a heavy tent stake, one that Kris Kringle had dropped from his bundle on the way to the cliff dweller's home.

The lad breathed a prayer of thankfulness and crept on with renewed courage.

He proceeded as far as he dared; then, lay still, listening for the noise of the expected conflict between the guide and the other red man.

It came. The sound was like that of a body falling heavily.

Once more the Indian at the table turned his head, listening inquiringly. He made a half motion to rise, glanced at the table, then sat down again and began to eat.

"His appetite has overcome his judgment," grinned Tad. The lad could hear the faint sound of conflict somewhere to the rear of him. He was getting uneasy and began to fidget.

All at once the red man sprang up, starting on a run, trailing Stacy's rifle behind him. He was headed directly for the place where Tad lay flattened on the ground, though the lad felt sure his enemy did not see him.

But when the Indian suddenly sprang up into the air to avoid stepping on the object that lay there, Tad knew that further secrecy was useless. The redskin had jumped right over him, dropping Chunky's rifle as he leaped. The gun fell on the Pony Rider boy and for a second hindered his movements.

But Tad was up like a flash, while the Indian whirled no less quickly, knife unsheathed, ready for battle.

This was where Tad's tent stake came in handy. Without it he would have been in a much more serious fix. It was bad enough as it was.

Without an instant's hesitation the lad brought the stake down on the wrist of the hand that held the knife. The knife fell to the ground, while the Indian, with a half-suppressed howl, sprang at the slender lad. Though the fellow's wrist was well-nigh useless at that moment, he was as full of fight as ever.

Tad stepped nimbly aside and tried to trip his adversary, but the Indian was too sharp to be caught that way.

"If he ever gets those arms around me I'm a goner," thought Tad, taking mental measure of his antagonist.

Suddenly the Indian swooped down, making a grab for the rifle that he had dropped.

As the redskin stooped, Tad hit him a wallop on the head with the tent stake. It must have made the savage see a shower of stars.

At least, it staggered him so he was glad to let the weapon remain where it was. For a few seconds the air was full of flying legs and arms, during which the boy landed three times on the red man, being himself unhurt.

Then the Indian succeeded in rushing into a clinch, and Tad found himself gripped in those arms of steel. Wriggle and twist as he would he could not free himself from their embrace. His adversary, on the other hand, found himself fully occupied in holding on to his slippery young antagonist, giving him neither time nor opportunity effectually to dispose of the slender lad.

Tad was unusually muscular for his years, to which was added no little skill as wrestler. The Indian soon discovered both these qualities. And, at about that time, the lad was resorting to every trick he knew to place the Indian in a position where he could be thrown.

The moment came with disconcerting suddenness, and Mr. Redman uttered a loud grunt as he landed on the ground, flat on his back. With a spring he lifted himself up, and the next instant he had thrown the slight figure of the Pony Rider Boy so heavily that everything about Tad grew black. He felt himself going. Then all at once he lost consciousness.

When finally he awakened, Tad found a figure still bending over him.

Quick as a flash the boy's arms went up, encircling the neck of the man kneeling by him. The next instant the fellow was on his back, with Tad sitting on his chest.

"Here, here! What's the matter with you?" gasped a muffled voice, which Tad instantly recognized.

"Kris Kringle!" he gasped.

"Yes; and you nearly knocked the breath out of me," grinned the guide, struggling to his feet. "Well, you certainly are a whirlwind."

"I—I thought you were the Indian," mattered Tad in a sheepish tone.

"If it had been, there would have been no need for my interference."

"Where is he?"

"Over there, tied up. Both of them are. We'll decide what to do with them when we get the party together."

"Tell me what happened," begged Tad.

The other fellow was so busy watching the cave that he forgot to keep his ears open. I was able to approach him without being detected. When I got near enough I laid the butt of my rifle over his head. No, I didn't hurt him much. Just made him curl up on the ground long enough to enable me to tie his hands and feet.

"About that time I caught the sound of something going on over here. I made a run, suspecting that you were mixing it up with the other redskin. Guess I was just in time, too, for he had you down and was reaching for something—"

"His knife," nodded Tad. "It's somewhere around here now."

"Well, I gave him the same medicine that I had given the other. Now we'd better go and call the others."

"Thank you. I'd have been in a bad fix, if you hadn't come as you did."

"So might I, had you not stopped the second one. We're quits then," said the guide, extending his hand, which Tad grasped warmly.

"I'll call the others, if you wish."

"Yes."

Tad ran over to the base of the cliff, and shouted loudly for his companions. In half an hour the party had gathered about the camp fire, engaged in an animated discussion over the stirring experiences of the evening.

It was decided that the Indians should be placed on their ponies, to which they were to be tied, with hands free and provisions enough to last them until they reached their reservation in the northern part of the state.

The guide restored their rifles to them after first taking their ammunition and transferring it to his own kit.

"I've wasted nearly that much on you," he said. "And, if ever you ride across my trail again, I'll use your own lead on you in a way that will stop you. You won't need bullets like these in the Happy Hunting Grounds, where you'll be going. Now, git!"

And they did. The redskins rode as if a ghost were pursuing them.

"That's the last, we shall see of those gentlemen," laughed Kris Kringle. "To-morrow morning we shall be on our way in peace."

But the trail of the Pony Rider Boys was not to be all peace. Before them—ere they reached the end of the Silver Trail—they were to find other thrilling experiences awaiting them.

CHAPTER XX.
TILTING FOR THE SILVER SPURS

Their journey led the young horsemen across the plains, over low-lying ranges, across broad, barren table-lands and down through the bottom lands until the wide sweep of the Rio Grande River at last lay before them.

After the weeks of arid landscape the sight of water, and so much of it, brought a loud cheer from the Pony Rider Boys. The next thing was to find a fording place. This they did late in the afternoon of the same day, and their further journey took them to the little desert town of Puraje.

They camped on the outskirts of the village.

"Here's where we get a real bath. Who's going in swimming with me?" asked Tad.

"I am," shouted all the boys at once.

The Professor and Kris Kringle concluded that they, too, would take a dip, and a merry hour was spent in a protected cove of the big river, where the boys proved themselves as much at home as they were in the saddle.

In the evening, they purchased such supplies as the town afforded. The night passed with-out disturbance, the boys taking up their journey next morning before the sleepy town had awakened.

It was a week later, when, tired and dusty, the outfit pulled up at La Luz, a quaint hamlet nestling in the foothills of the Sacramento Mountains. The place they found to be largely Mexican, and it was almost as if the visitors had slipped over the border to find themselves in Mexico itself.

Decorations were in evidence on all sides; bright-colored mantillas, Indian blankets and flags were everywhere.

"Hello, I guess something is going on here," laughed Tad.

"We are in time, whatever it is," nodded the guide. "Probably it's a feast of some kind. You will be interested in it, if that is what it is."

The feast, they learned, was to be celebrated on the morrow with games, feats of strength and horsemanship.

"Do you think they will let us take part?" asked Tad, as the party made camp in the yard of a little adobe church, where they had obtained permission to camp.

"I'll see about it," answered the guide. "There may be reasons why it would not be best to do so."

"Maybe I can win another rifle," suggested Chunky.

"These people don't give away rifles. They're too— too—what do you call it?—too artistic. That's it."

The camp being on the main street of the village, attracted no little attention. After sundown, crowds of gayly bedecked young people strolled up and stood about the church yard, watching the American boys pitching their tents and preparing for their stay over night.

The villagers were especially interested in watching the boys get their supper, which was served up steaming hot within fifteen minutes after preparations had begun. Chunky had bought several pies at the store, which, with a pound of cheese brought in by Ned, made a pleasant change in the daily routine.

Chunky started in on the pie.

Ned calmly reached over and took it away from him; then the supper went along until it came time for the dessert, when Chunky fixed his eyes on the cheese suspiciously.

"See anything wrong with that cheese?" demanded Ned.

"No, but I've got an idea."

"Out with it! You won't rest easy until you do. What's your idea?"

"I was thinking, if I had a camera, I could make a motion picture of that cheese. I heard of a fellow once—"

"That will do, Master Stacy," warned Professor Zepplin.

"Can't I talk?"

"Along proper lines—yes."

"Cheese is proper, isn't it?"

"Depends upon how old it is," chuckled Tad.

"You needn't make fun of my cheese. Here give it to me; I'll eat it."

"You're welcome to it, Ned," laughed the boys.

The fun went on, much to the amusement of the villagers, who remained near by until the evening was well along and the lads began preparing for bed. Next morning the visitors began coming in to town early. There were men from the ranches, Mexican ranch-hands arrayed in bright colors and displaying expensive saddle trimmings. There were others from the wild places on the desert, far beyond the water limits, whose means of livelihood were known only to themselves.

It was a strange company, and one that appealed considerably to the curiosity of the Pony Rider Boys.

The early part of the day was given over to racing, roping, gambling and other sports in which the lads were content to take no part. But there was an event scheduled for the afternoon that interested Tad more than all the rest. That was a tilting bout, open to all comers. A tilting arch had been erected in the middle of the main street, and had been decorated with flags and greens.

The tilting ring, suspended from the top of the arch, was not more than an inch in diameter. The horseman who could impale it on his tilting peg and carry the ring away with him the greatest, number of times, would be declared the winner. Each one was to be given five chances.

The prize, a pair of silver spurs, was to be presented by the belle of the town, a dark-eyed señorita.

The guide had entered Tad in this contest; but, as the lad glanced up at the ring only an inch in diameter, he grew rather dubious. He never had seen any tilting, and did not even know how the sport was conducted.

Kris Kringle gave the lad some instructions about the method employed by the tilters, and Tad decided to enter the contest.

Only ten horsemen entered, most of these being either Mexicans or halfbreeds.

The first trial over, five of the contestants had succeeded in carrying away the ring. Tad had waited until nearly the last in order to get all the information possible as to the way the rest of the contestants played the game. A pole had been loaned to him, or rather a "peg," they called it, eight feet long, tapered so as to allow it to go through the brass ring for fully two feet of its length.

The Pony Rider boy took his place in the middle of the street, and without the least hesitancy, galloped down toward the ring, which, indeed, he could not even see. When within a few feet of the arch he caught the sparkle of the ring.

His lance came up, and putting spurs to his broncho, he shot under the arch, driving the point of the peg full at the slender circle. The point struck the edge sending the ring swaying like the pendulum of a clock.

A howl greeted his achievement. Tad said nothing, but riding slowly back, awaited his next trial.

The rule was that when one of the contestants made a strike, he was to continue until he failed. He would be allowed to run out five points in succession if he could.

"Rest the peg against your side, and lightly," advised a man, as Tad turned into the street for another try. The man was past middle age, and, though dressed in the garb of a man of the plains, Tad decided at once that he was not of the same type as most of the motley mob by which he was surrounded.

The lad nodded his understanding.

With a sharp little cry of warning, the boy put spurs to his pony. He fairly flew down the course. No such speed had been seen there that day. The northern bronchos that the boys were riding were built for faster work and possessed more spirit than their brothers of the desert.

As he neared the arch, this time, the lad half rose in his stirrups. He knew where to look for the ring now. Leaning slightly forward he let the point of the peg tilt ever so little. It went through the ring, tearing it from its slender fastening and carrying it away.

Loud shouts of approval greeted his achievement.

Once more he raced down the lane, this time at so fast a clip that the faces of the spectators who lined the course were a mere blur in his eyes.

He felt the slight jar and heard the click as the ring slipped over the tilting peg.

"Two," announced the scorer.

He missed the next one. Then the others took their turn. Only one of these succeeded in scoring. He was one of the Mexicans who made such a brave show of color in raiment and saddle cloth.

"That gives the señor and the boy three apiece. Each has one turn left. The others will fall out. If neither scores in his turn, both will be ruled out and the others will compete for the prize," announced the scorer.

The Mexican smiled a supercilious smile, as much as to say, "The idea of a long-legged, freckle-faced boy defeating me!" The Mexican was an expert at the game of tilting as it was practised on the desert.

The man took the first turn. He sat quietly on his pony a moment before starting, placing the lance at just the proper angle—then galloped at the mark. He, too, rose in his stirrups. The spectators were silent.

The ring just missed being impaled on the tilting peg, slipping along the pole half way then bounding up into the air.

The spectators groaned. The Mexican had lost.

Now it was Tad's turn.

He rode as if it were an everyday occurrence with him to tilt, only he went at it with a rash that fairly took their breath away.

Just as he was about to drive at the ring, some one uttered a wild yell and a sombrero hurled from the crowd, struck Tad fairly across the eyes.

Of course he lost, and, for a moment, he could not see a thing. He pulled his pony to a quick stop and sat rubbing and blinking his smarting eyes.

A howl of disapproval went up from the spectators. None seemed to know whether the act had been inspired by enthusiasm or malice. Tad was convinced that it was the latter. His face was flushed, but the lad made no comment.

"You are entitled to another tilt," called the scorer.

To this the Mexican objected loudly.

"Under the circumstances, as my opponent objects, and as we all wish to prevent hard feelings, why not give him a chance as well? If he wins I shall be satisfied."

A shout of approval greeted Tad's suggestion. This was the real sportsman-like spirit, and it appealed to them.

The proposition was agreed to. But again the Mexican lost.

"If the young man is interfered with this time, I shall award the prize to him and end the tournament," warned the scorer.

Though Tad's eyes were smarting from the blow of the sombrero, he allowed the eyelids to droop well over them, thus protecting them from the dust and at the same time giving him a clearer vision.

On his next turn, Tad tore down the narrow lane; he shot between the posts like an arrow, and the tilting peg was driven far into the narrow hoop, wedging the ring on so firmly that it afterwards required force to loosen and remove it.

Without halting his pony, Tad rode on, out a circle and came back at a lively gallop, pulling up before the stand of dry goods boxes, where the young woman who was to award the prize stood swinging her handkerchief, while the spectators set up a deafening roar of applause.

Tad was holding the tilting peg aloft, displaying the ring wedged on it. He made the young woman a sweeping bow, his sombrero almost touching the ground as he did so.

Another shout went up when the handsome spurs were handed to him, which the enthusiastic young woman first wrapped in her own handkerchief before passing the prize over to him. And amid the din, Tad heard the familiar "Oh, Wow! Wow!" in the shrill voice of Stacy Brown.

CHAPTER XXI.
THE FAT BOY'S DISCOVERY

"I saw him! I saw him, Tad!"

"Saw who, Chunky?"

"I tell you, I did. Don't you s'pose I know what my eyes tell me in confidence. Don't you to go to contradicting to me."

Stacy had fairly overwhelmed Tad Butler with the importance of his discovery; but, thus far, Tad had not the least idea what it was all about.

"When you get quieted down perhaps you'll be good enough to tell me who it is you saw?"

"The man, the man!"

"Humph! That's about as clear as the water in an alkali sink. What man?"

"The one we saw on the train. Don't you know?"

Tad thought a moment.

"You mean the one we heard talking just before we got to Bluewater?" Butler had entirely forgotten the incident.

"Yes; that's him! That's him," exploded Stacy.

"You say that fellow—Lasar, that's his name—is he here!"

"Uh-huh."

"Where?"

"He got off the stage down by the postoffice, just when I was coming up here."

"Was he alone?"

"The other fellow wasn't with him, if that's what you mean?"

"Yes." Tad went over in his mind the conversation the man Lasar had held with his companion, in which the pair were plotting against some one by the name of Marquand.

"Oh, well, Chunky, it's none of our concern. I think we must have magnified the incident. I—"

"He'll bear watching, Tad. He will and it's muh— muh—you understand who's going to do it," declared Chunky, swelling out his chest and tapping it with his right fist.

"All right, go ahead," laughed Tad. "It's time some of us get into more trouble. The Professor will begin to think we've got a fever, or something, if we let two days in succession pass without stirring up something."

"I've got an idea," exploded Stacy.

"There you go. It's coming now."

"I'll go tell the policeman."

"Why, you ninny, there are no policemen here. Perhaps there is a sheriff. Hello, here comes the gentleman who gave me the advice that helped me to win those handsome spurs. He's introducing himself to the Professor and Mr. Kringle. Let's go over."

Forgetting for the moment the subject they were discussing, Tad and Stacy strolled over to the camp-fire.

"O Tad, this is Mr. Marquand, Mr. James Marquand from Albuquerque. He wants to know you. And this is another one of our Pony Rider Boys, Master Stacy Brown," said the Professor, presenting his boys.

"Marquand!" exclaimed both boys under their breaths.

"I am glad to know you, Master Butler. That was a very fine piece of work you did this afternoon. You've steady nerves."

"If there's any credit due it is to you. Your suggestion helped me to win the prize. Without it I should have failed," answered Tad generously.

"Which way are you headed?" asked Mr. Marquand.

"Guadalupes," answered the guide. "The boys want to explore some of the old pueblos."

"And I also," spoke up Professor Zepplin. "I understand there is much of interest in them."

"I should say so," muttered their guest.

"I'd like a few moments to speak with you in private, if you can spare the time," said Tad in a low voice, at the first opportunity.

"At your service now, sir."

"No; not here."

"Then come to my room at the hotel. I'll fix it with the others," said Mr. Marquand, observing at once that the lad had some serious purpose in mind.

"My friend Chunky will go with me, if agreeable to you?"

"That's all right. Professor, if you have no objection I should like to have these two young men go to my quarters with me for a little while. I—"

"Certainly. Don't stay out too late, boys."

"No, sir."

"Wonder what they've got up their sleeves?" muttered Ned, watching the receding figures of his two companions and Mr. Marquand.

"You may talk," smiled the latter after they were well started.

"I'd rather not until we are where we shall not be overheard," answered Tad promptly.

All three fell silent. The boys followed their host to his room, apparently without having been observed. The little village was too full of its own pleasures to notice.

"Be seated, boys. I take for granted that neither of you smoke?"

"Oh no, sir."

"Now, what can I do for you? I am sure you have something of importance to yourselves on your minds."

"Not to us specially. Perhaps to you, though," replied Tad.

"Indeed?"

"We may be foolish. If so, you will understand that we have no motive beyond a desire to serve you."

"That goes without saying."

"Do you know a man by the name of Lasar—Bob Lasar, Mr. Marquand?"

Mr. Marquand started, eyeing both lads questioningly.

"Yes; he is associated with me in a business venture."

"Told you so," interjected Stacy.

"What of him?"

Tad wished he was well out of it all. To be obliged to tell all he knew of Bob Lasar, and to the latter's partner, was rather a troublesome undertaking.

Plucking up courage, Tad briefly related all that he and his companion had overheard on the train as they were approaching Bluewater to all of which their host listened with grave attention and increasing interest.

"The incident probably would not have come back to me again but for certain things that happened to-day," Tad continued.

"Would either of you know Lasar were you to see him again, do you think?"

"My friend Chunky Brown saw him here to-day."

"Saw him get out of the stage in front of this very hotel," nodded Stacy.

"You are right. He is here. Mr. Lasar had stopped off at a near-by town on a personal matter. Can you describe the man whom you saw with him on the train?"

"As I remember him, he was slightly taller than Mr. Lasar, with red hair and a moustache of the same shade."

"Yes, that's Joe Comstock. No doubt about that," nodded Mr. Marquand. "You didn't hear them say what their plan was, then?"

"Not definitely. Only that they intended to rid themselves of you after having obtained possession of your plans for finding the treasure, or at least learning where it is hidden."

"Hm-m-m!"

Mr. Marquand sat thoughtfully silent for several minutes, the lines of his face growing tense and hard. The boys could see that he was exerting, a strong effort to control himself.

"You—you haven't told them your plans?" questioned Tad, in a subdued voice.

"No. I was going to do so to-night, if Comstock had arrived. He may get in yet."

"But you won't do so now—will you?"

"No! I thank you, boys," exclaimed their host, extending an impulsive hand to each at the same time.

"Then—then our information *is* going to be of some use to you?"

"More than you can have any idea of. You have done me a greater service than you know. I thank you—thank you from the bottom of my heart! Perhaps, ere long I may be able to show my appreciation in a more substantial manner."

Marquand ceased speaking abruptly and began pacing back and forth, hands thrust deep into his coat pockets. He was a man of slight build, but strong and wiry. He was well past middle age, erect and forceful. Looking at him, Tad found himself wondering how such a man could have gotten into the clutches of two such rascals as Bob Lasar and Joe Comstock. Tad hoped their host would offer some explanation, while Chunky was nearly bursting with curiosity. Mr. Marquand appeared to have forgotten their presence entirely.

"I think we had better be going now," suggested Tad, rising.

"Wait!" commanded their host. "Sit down! I have something to say to you. Then, perhaps, I'll walk back to your camp and have a talk with the Professor. What sort of man is your guide?"

"He's a very fine man—"

"That's my idea. What you heard on the train is borne out by several little things that have come under my observation within the last few days, but I did not think they would go as far as you have indicated. I will tell you frankly, that I expect the treasure which we hope to find to be a big one. How I happened to take these men in with me, in the search for it, is unnecessary to state. However, I am done with them, now, for good. They know that I have not put my information on paper, or else they might have made an end of me before this."

"Is the treasure near this vicinity, Mr. Marquand?" asked Tad.

"About two days' journey. I expect to find it at or near the ruins of an old Pueblo house. You know they built their homes one on top of another. Some of their adobe houses are six and seven stories high. Even if we locate the place, we may experience great difficulty in finding that of which we are in search. How would you boys like to join me? It will be an interesting experience for you?"

"Help—help you find the buried treasure?" questioned Chunky, his face red with suppressed excitement.

"Yes."

"Great!" chorused the lads.

"I'll talk with Professor Zepplin. Come, we will go over to the camp now."

When Mr. Marquand and the Professor had finished their conference, Tad and Chunky leaned forward eagerly to learn the result.

"Yes," nodded Mr. Marquand; "you're all going to help me find the ancient Pueblo treasure."

CHAPTER XXII.
IN HAND-TO-HAND CONFLICT

"I'm done with you, Bob Lasar! And you, too, Comstock!" thundered Mr. Marquand, as the rascals stood at the door of his room some two hours later.

Mr. Marquand had been waiting for them, and with him was Tad Butler, whom he had urged to accompany him back to the hotel that he might be a witness to what took place. Perhaps, too, Mr. Marquand reasoned that his former associates might not take the same attitude toward him in the presence of the boy that they might otherwise take.

The two men had halted in the doorway as Mr. Marquand hurled his decision at them.

Lasar shoved his companion into the room and closed the door.

"Sit down, both of you! So you thought to hoodwink me—to get the secret of the treasure and then put me out of the way, eh? That was your game, was it? Well, it's all off now. I'll have nothing further to do with you."

"Why—why, Mr. Marquand, it's all a mistake!" began one of the pair.

"Perhaps you'll deny having plotted against me on a train on your way to Bluewater."

"I deny ever having tried to put up a game on—"

"Master Tad, did you ever see these men before?"

They turned on the lad quickly. Neither man had previously observed him.

"Yes, sir."

"Where?"

"On the train, as you mentioned just now."

"And they were plotting my life?"

"So it seemed to me, sir."

"What have you to say to that?" demanded Mr. Marquand.

"That the boy lies!"

Tad's face flushed angrily.

"That'll do," said Marquand, more quietly.

"Then you believe him—you do not believe me?"

"I believe him. I know he has told me the truth. Now, it isn't necessary to explain to you. You deserve no explanation and you'll get none further than what you already have."

"But—"

"No 'buts' about it. I said I was done with you. Now, I want you to get out of my sight! You're a couple of rogues—so crooked that you can't walk straight."

Bob Lasar's face had grown livid with rage. His anger was rapidly getting beyond all bounds. Tad observed it and saw the storm coming. It arrived a moment later when Lasar whipped out a revolver.

Before Mr. Marquand could make a move to draw his own weapon Bob had aimed his weapon and pulled the trigger.

Tad, instantly divining the purpose of the man when he saw his hand fly to the pistol holster under his coat, sprang forward.

There was a deafening report. A bullet buried itself in the ceiling of the room.

Tad had struck up the desperado's arm just in the nick of time, thus preventing a terrible crime. But the end was not yet. There were five more bullets in the cylinder of the weapon, as the lad knew full well.

He grabbed Lasar's arm, hanging on desperately, at the same time trying to get a wrestling hold.

The weapon went off again, this time sending a bullet into the floor.

"Look out for the other fellow!" shouted Tad.

Mr. Marquand already had done so. Comstock had just made an attempt to draw his own weapon when Marquand threw himself upon the man. The two went crashing to the floor, while Tad and

Lasar were battling all over the room, the latter's weapon barking viciously every little while.

Lasar was much more powerful than his slender antagonist, but Tad being very quick on his feet managed to keep out of the way of the revolver and at the same time to avoid being thrown.

Suddenly, the boy gave the gun-hand of his opponent a quick twist.

Lasar uttered a sharp exclamation of pain. The revolver clattered to the floor.

Quick as a flash, Tad threw a leg behind the knee of his antagonist, gave it a quick jerk, with the result that Lasar went to the floor with great violence.

By this time, occupants of the hotel were running down the hall, while others were hammering at the door. Lasar had turned the key upon entering the room.

Those within did not have time to listen to the demands of those in the hall, who were demanding admission.

Mr. Marquand, as soon as he got his opponent down, quickly disarmed him.

"Get up!" he commanded. "I don't want to kill you. I ought to do so, but I won't."

He sprang from Comstock, and jerking Tad from Lasar, whom the lad was making heroic efforts to hold down, pulled the fallen rascal to his feet.

"Get out, both of you!" he commanded, covering both his visitors with his weapon.

Lasar, in struggling to his feet, reached for his revolver.

"Drop it or I'll fill you full of lead!"

At that instant, the door burst open and half a dozen men sprang into the room.

Lasar, seeing that he was caught, leaped through the open window. He was followed closely by Comstock. He, too, made a clean leap, landing on the soft ground below.

"What's the meaning of this shooting?" shouted the proprietor, his face flushed with anger.

"Two men tried to murder me," replied Marquand coolly.

"It looks as though you were doing your share of it," snapped the proprietor, noting his guest's belligerent attitude and drawn weapon.

Just then three shots in quick succession were fired from the outside. Two of the bullets narrowly missed some of the men, who had forced their way into the room.

As the third shot was fired, Tad threw one hand to his head; then drew it away grinning.

"Those rascals have evidently gotten a new supply of fire arms," he said.

A bullet had gone through his hair and his scalp burned where the lead had brushed it.

All of the newcomers drew their revolvers and sprang to the window.

"Don't shoot!" cried the Pony Rider Boy; "You'll hit the wrong one. There are a hundred people down there."

"He's right!" shouted Mr. Marquand, pushing his way between the men and the window, at the imminent risk of getting a bullet in his back from either Lasar or Comstock. "Let 'em go. They'll be running for home about this time. They are a couple of scoundrels, sir."

"But the damage. Look at my fine room."

"I'll pay for the damage, and I'll quit your hotel now. I've had enough of the place," retorted Mr. Marquand, pulling a roll of bills from his pocket. "How much is it?"

"Well, you see—"

"How much is it?"

"Well, I guess twenty-five would be about right. You see—"

"Here's your twenty-five. Clear out!"

With many apologies the proprietor, accompanied by the others, backed from the room.

"We came pretty near having a fight, didn't we?" Marquand smiled, looking at Tad for the first time since the disturbance began.

"Almost."

"He would have got me if you hadn't knocked up his gun-hand. That's another one I owe you. Well, maybe we'll have a pay day soon."

"You had better go back to camp with me, and bunk in with us tonight," suggested the lad, "We shall want to make an early start in the morning, anyway. I think it will be safer there, too. That pair won't dare come fooling around our camp, knowing they can't trifle with us," added the lad, with a note of pride in his tone.

"I'll do it. Not that I'm afraid of anything that walks on two legs, but the sooner we hitch up the better it'll be. Got room enough?"

"Plenty. Where's your pony?"

"Up near your camp. Come on."

The man and the boy walked from the hotel, the former looking neither to the right nor to the left, Tad observing their surroundings half suspiciously. He was sure they had not yet heard the last of Bob Lasar and Joe Comstock. In this he was right.

Marquand and the boy had gone no more than ten rods from the hotel, when the report of a revolver was heard, and a bullet fired from the corner of an adobe building passed within an inch of Mr. Marquand's head.

With wonderful quickness the latter drew and sent three shots at the flash.

Whether he had hit any thing or not he did not know.

"Run! I don't want you to get hit," cried the boy's new friend, grasping Tad by the hand and starting off at a brisk pace.

"Bullets don't scare me, so long as they don't hit me," laughed young Butler.

CHAPTER XXIII.
MOONBEAM POINTS THE WAY

"The moon will be here in a moment."

"What was it the old Pueblo chief said, Mr. Marquand?"

"'When the full of the moon has come and shoots its first arrow over the crests of the Guadalupes, it points the way to the treasure of my ancient people,'" quoted Mr. Marquand.

"I presume that would be taken to mean that, at a certain phase of the moon, one of its beams points to where the treasure is hidden," explained Professor Zepplin. "But what leads you to believe this is the Pueblo village of your particular chief's ancestors?"

"Yes; I don't see why it might not be any of the ruined adobe houses in this valley?" said Ned Rector.

They had journeyed rapidly over mountain and plain to the valley of the Guadalupes, where Mr. Marquand had informed them that he expected to find the treasure. In the three days consumed on the journey, the travelers had seen nothing of either Lasar or Comstock. Evidently the pair had decided to leave the country while they still had the chance, fearing that perhaps Mr. Marquand might invoke the aid of the law to rid himself of them if they remained.

The Pony Rider Boys and their outfit had arrived that afternoon, and during the remaining hours of daylight they had been excitedly exploring the ancient dwellings, most of which were in a dilapidated condition. There was one, however, two stories in height, that was in an excellent state of preservation. In fact it appeared as if it had only recently been vacated. After an examination of all the ruins Mr. Marquand had discovered what led him to believe that this was the structure which the old Pueblo chief referred to in his description of the resting place of the treasure. The chief had said he had never been near the spot. He was the only member of his tribe to whom the secret had been handed down, and he in turn had transmitted it to the white man who now stood within the shadow of the ancient dwelling place.

"I have my reasons for believing this is the place," answered Mr. Marquand, in response to the Professor's question. "If I am wrong, we shall have to wait until the moon rises to-morrow night. Come inside now, and we will close the door."

All hands crowded into the cool chamber, closing the heavy wooden door that barred the entrance.

"Don't see how moonlight can get through solid walls," muttered Stacy. "Ought to leave the door open."

No one answered him. In the darkened chamber, with its peculiar, musty odors, the boys did not feel in the mood for hilarity or even for speech. There was something about their situation that seemed to impress them profoundly.

"Stand over against the wall on the side, so as not to obstruct any light that might possibly get in here," directed Mr. Marquand.

The others moved silently to the side of the room indicated by him. They had stood thus for fully five minutes when an exclamation from Stacy broke the stillness harshly.

"Look! Look!" cried the fat boy.

A slender shaft of light had suddenly pierced the blackness, coming they knew not whence. It was there.

"Must be a pin hole through the wall up near the ceiling," suggested Kris Kringle.

The silver thread shot across the chamber, ending abruptly on the adobe floor some three feet from the back wall.

"That's the spot!" shouted Mr. Marquand triumphantly.

He threw himself on the floor, and with his knife scratched a cross on the spot where the moonbeam rested. Scarcely had he done so when the delicate shaft of light disappeared as suddenly as it had come.

"It's gone," breathed the boys.

"But it has pointed the way."

"And we have followed the silver trail to its end," added Ned Rector poetically.

"Bring the tools!" cried Mr. Marquand.

While they were doing so, he struck a match and lighted the lantern that they had brought with them from their camp in the foothills. His first care was to bar the door with the heavy wooden timber that he had cut and which he now slipped into its fastenings.

A close examination of the floor revealed no marks save those put there by the treasure-hunter's knife.

"This house seems to be built on the solid ground. I do not think you will find anything under it," protested the Professor.

"There are houses under every one of these buildings," answered Mr. Marquand. He held a short, keen edged bar in place, while Kris Kringle swung the maul. Gradually they cut a ring about two feet in diameter about the cross. The material of which the floor had been made had been tempered with the years and was almost as hard as flint.

The steady thud of the heavy maul, accompanied by the click, click of the cutting bar, the dim light, the silent, expectant faces, formed a weird picture in this silent desert place.

After a full half hour of this the two men paused, and stood back, drawing sleeves across their foreheads to wipe away the perspiration.

Stacy Brown walked pompously over to the circle.

"Maybe I can fall through it. If I can't, nobody can," he said, jumping up and down on the spot where they had been cutting.

There followed a rambling sound, and with a yell, Stacy Brown suddenly disappeared from sight. In place of the circle in which he had been standing was a black, ragged hole, from which particles of the mortar were still crumbling and rattling to the bottom of the pit.

"Are you there?" cried Kris Kringle, leaping to the spot, thrusting the lantern down through the opening. "Master Stacy!"

"Wow!" responded the boy from the depths.

"Did it hurt you?"

"How far did you fall?"

This and other questions were hurled at the fat boy, as his companions crowded about the opening.

"I'm killed. That'll answer all your questions," replied Stacy. "Hurry up! Get my remains out of this place."

The rays of the lantern disclosed a short stairway, built of the same material of which the house itself had been constructed.

Mr. Marquand forced himself past the guide and was down the steps in a twinkling. He was followed by the wondering Pony Rider Boys, Professor Zepplin and Kris Kringle in short order, for all crowded down through the narrow opening.

Chunky had hit the top step and rolled all the way down. He had scrambled to his feet and was rubbing his shins by the time his friends reached him. His clothes were torn and he was covered with dust.

"Fell down the cellar, didn't I?" he grinned.

But no one gave any heed to him now. Mr. Marquand had snatched at the lantern and was running from point to point of the chamber in which they found themselves. He was laboring under great excitement.

"Here's another opening," he shouted. "We haven't got to the bottom yet."

Another flight of stairs led to still another and smaller chamber below. Mr. Marquand let out a yell the moment he reached the bottom. The others rushed pell-mell after him.

There, with it's top just showing above the dirt was a long iron chest.

"Give me the maul!" shouted the excited treasure seeker.

He attacked the rusty iron fastenings; at last the cover yielded to his thunderous blows and falling on its edge, toppled over to the floor with a crash.

"Somebody's old clothes," chuckled Stacy, peering into the open chest.

The garments, priestly robes that lay at the top, fell to pieces the instant Mr. Marquand laid violent hands on them.

"Look! Look! Was I right or was I wrong?" he cried, beside himself with joy.

There, before their astonished eyes, lay a chest of gold— coins dulled by age, small nuggets and chunks of silver, all heaped indiscriminately in the treasure chest.

"I did it!" shouted Chunky. "I did it with my little feet! I fell in and discovered the treasure!"

The tongues of the Pony Rider Boys were suddenly loosened. Such a shout as they set up probably never had been heard before in the ancient adobe mansion of the Pueblos. Cheer after cheer echoed through the chambers and reached the ears of a dozen desperadoes who were skulking amid the sage brush without.

Professor Zepplin scooped up a handful of the coins and examined them under the lantern.

"Old Spanish coins," he informed them. "Pure gold. And look at these nuggets! Where do you suppose the Indians found them?"

"There are hidden mines in the State," informed Mr. Marquand. "Some of these days they will be discovered. I have been hunting for them myself, but without success. Boys, what do you think of it now? If it had not been for you I might never have seen this sight."

Their eyes were fairly bulging as they gazed at the heap of gold. Chunky squatted down scooping up a double handful and letting the coins run through his fingers. Then the other boys dipped in, laughing for pure joy, more because their adventure had borne fruit than for the love of the gold itself.

"Must be more'n a bushel of it," announced Stacy.

"Those old Franciscans must have been saving up for a rainy day. And it never rained here at all," suggested Ned humorously.

"Shall we count it?" asked Mr. Marquand.

"Just as you wish," replied the Professor.

"Were I in your place, Mr. Marquand, I should get the stuff out of here as soon as possible. You can't tell what may happen. I would suggest that we secure the treasure and be on our way at once. You will want to get it to a bank as quickly as possible. This is one of the things that cannot be kept quiet."

"You are right. Will somebody go over to the camp and get those gunny sacks of mine? I don't want to lose sight of my find for a minute. You know how I feel about it—not that I do not trust you. You know—"

"Surely we understand," smiled Tad.

"And you all have an interest in it—you shall share the treasure with me—"

"No, we don't," shouted the boys. "We've had more than a million dollars worth of fun out of it already."

"Certainly not," added the Professor.

"We'll discuss that later," said Mr. Marquand firmly. "Just now we must take care of what we have found. Who will get the bags?"

"We will," answered the boys promptly.

"No; you stay here. I'll get them," answered Kris Kringle. "Light me up the stairs so I don't break my neck in this old rookery."

One of the boys lighted the way to the next floor, then stepped back into the cellar, where Mr. Marquand was turning over the treasure in an effort to find out if the pile extended all the way to the bottom of the chest.

In the meantime Kris Kringle unbarred the door and threw it part way open. He did it cautiously, as if half expecting trouble.

He threw the door to with a bang, springing to one side, and dropping the bar back into place.

The reason for his sudden change of plans was that no sooner had the door opened than several thirty-eight calibre bullets were fired from the sage brush outside.

Kris Kringle waited to learn whether those in the cellar had heard the shots. But they had not. They were some distance below ground, and their minds were wholly taken up with the great treasure before them.

After a few moments the guide once more removed the bar, first having drawn his revolver in case of sudden surprise. Then he cautiously opened the door an inch or so.

At first nothing happened. The moonlit landscape lay as silent and peaceful as if there were not a human being on the desert.

There were six distinct flashes all at once and a rain of lead showered into the door.

Kris Kringle took a pot shot at one of the flashes, then slammed the door shut and barred it.

"Well; I hope that would get you," he muttered.

Hastily retracing his steps he called the party up to the second cellar.

"Did you fetch the sacks?" called Mr. Marquand.

"No, but I've fetched trouble. It's coming in sackfuls."

"What do you mean?"

"We're besieged."

"Besieged?" wondered the Professor.

"Yes; there's a crowd outside, and they've been trying to shoot me up. Must be some of your friends, Mr. Marquand."

"Lasar and Comstock? The scoundrels!" growled Mr. Marquand. "But we'll make short work of them."

"Not so easy as you think There are more than two out there— there's a crowd and they've got rifles. Our rifles are over in the camp. I've got a six-shooter and so have you, but what do they amount to against half a dozen rifles?"

"I'll talk to them, if I can get any place to make them hear," announced Mr. Marquand, starting up the stairs.

"I reckon there's a window on the second floor, but you'd better be careful that you don't get winged," warned the guide.

Mr. Marquand went right on, and the others followed. As the guide had said there was a small window on the floor above the ground, apparently the only one in the house.

Mr. Marquand hailed the besiegers.

"Who are you and what do you mean by shooting us up in this fashion?" he demanded.

"You ought to know who we are, Jim Marquand, and you know what we want!"

"Yes, I know you all right, Lasar, and I'll make you smart for this."

"The place is as much mine as it is yours," answered Lasar. "And I propose to take it! If you'll make an even divvy of what you have found, or expect to find, we'll go away and let you alone. If you don't we'll take the whole outfit."

"Take it, take it!" jeered Marquand. "You couldn't take it in a hundred years—not unless you used artillery."

"Then we'll starve you out," replied the man in the sage brush.

"Look out!" warned the guide.

Mr. Marquand sprang to one side just as a volley crashed through the opening, the bullets rattling to the floor after bounding back from the flint-like walls.

"I guess they've got you, Mr. Marquand. We can't hold out forever. If we had rifles we could pick them off by daylight. But when morning comes they'll draw back out of revolver range and plunk the first man who shows himself outside. Have you any title to this property?"

"Yes. I have bought up a hundred acres about here. The deeds are in my pocket. I guess nobody has a better title.".

"His title is all right," spoke up Professor Zepplin. "I made sure of that before I decided to come with Mr. Marquand."

"Then there's only one thing to be done."

"What's that?"

"Get a sheriff's posse and bag the whole bunch."

Mr. Marquand laughed harshly.

"If we were in a position to get a posse we should be able to get away without one. I think we had better go below. This is not a very safe place with this open window."

"I'll remain here."

"What for, Kringle?"

"Somebody's got to watch the front door to see that they don't play any tricks on us. It's clouding up, and if the night gets dark they'll try to get in."

"How far is it to a place where we could get a sheriff?" asked Tad, who had been thinking deeply.

"Hondo. Fifteen miles due east of here as the moon rises. Why?"

"If I were sure I could find my way, I think I might get some help," answered the lad quietly.

"You!" snapped Mr. Marquand, turning on him.

"If I had a rope. Perhaps I can do it without one."

"I'd like to know how?"

158 | The Pony Rider Boys in New Mexico; Or, The End of the Silver Trail

Mr. Marquand was inclined to treat the proposition lightly, believing that such a move as proposed by Tad Butler was an impossibility. Kris Kringle, however, was regarding the boy inquiringly. He knew that Tad had some plan in mind and that it was likely to be a good one.

"The rascals are all out in front of the house, aren't they?"

"Yes, Master Tad. There's no reason why they should be behind the house. They know we can't get out that way; because there is no opening on that side."

Tad nodded.

"Then I can do it."

"Tad, what foolish idea have you in mind now? I cannot consent to your taking any more chances."

"Professor, we are taking long enough chances as it is. Unless we are relieved soon, we shall be starved out and perhaps worse."

"What's your plan?" interrupted Kris Kringle.

"See that hole in the roof up there?" Tad pointed.

They had not seen it before, but they did now. A light suddenly dawned upon Kris Kringle.

"Boy, you are the only level-headed one in the outfit. You would have made a corking Indian fighter."

"I'm the Indian fighter," chimed in Stacy.

"You can boost me up to the hole and I'll go over the rear of the house, get to the camp and from there ride to Hondo."

Tad's three companions started a cheer, which the guide sternly put down.

"I can't consent to any such plan," decided the Professor sternly.

The rest reasoned with him until, finally, he did consent, though he knew the lad would be taking desperate chances. Tad understood that as well as the rest of them, but he was burning to be off.

Kris Kringle gave him careful directions as to how to get to the place.

"Take your rifle with you, if you can get it. After you get half a mile or a mile away shoot once. That will tell us you are all right."

"You can help me in getting away from here, if you will do some shooting to cover my escape," suggested Tad.

"That's a good idea," agreed the guide. "You wait on the roof until we begin to rake the sage with our revolvers. Then drop. Take a wide circuit, so that you won't stumble over the enemy."

Tad gave his belt a hitch, stuffed his sombrero under it and announced himself as ready.

The guide stepped under the hole. Tad quickly climbed to his shoulder and stood up like a circus performer. He could easily reach the roof with his hands. A second more and his feet were lifted from the shoulders of the guide. They saw the figure in the opening; then it disappeared.

A slight scraping noise was the only sound they heard.

Tad flattened himself out and wriggled along toward the rear of the roof. Peering over the edge he made sure that there was no one about. He then lay quietly waiting for the shooting to begin.

"Let 'em have it," directed Kris Kringle.

A sudden fusillade was emptied into the sage brush.

Tad swung himself over the edge of the roof, hung on for a few seconds, then dropped lightly to the ground.

CHAPTER XXIV.
CONCLUSION

The enemy answered the shots with a volley, and for a few moments a lot of ammunition was wasted while the odor of gunpowder assailed nostrils on both sides.

After that, the shooting died away. As the minutes lengthened into an hour, and no word of Tad's mission had been received, the defenders began to grow restless. They were under a double tension now. Mr. Marquand was pacing up and down the floor.

Suddenly, forgetful of the danger that lurked out there, he poked his head out of the window.

A sharp *pat* on the stone window frame beside him, after the bullet had snipped off the tip of his left ear, caused Mr. Marquand to draw back suddenly. He stalked about the floor, holding a handkerchief to the wounded ear, "talking in dashes and asterisks," as Chunky put it.

Kris Kringle's face wore a grim smile. He was taking chances of being shot, every second now, but he insisted in holding his place at the side of the window so he could listen and watch.

A thin, fleecy veil covered the moon, but it was not dense enough to fully hide objects on the landscape.

"All keep quiet, now," warned Kris Kringle. "We should get a signal pretty soon."

"I'm afraid something has happened to the boy," muttered the Professor. Then all fell silent.

"There it goes!" exclaimed the guide in a tone of great relief.

The crack of a rifle afar off sounded clear and distinct.

"He's made it. Thank heaven!" breathed Mr. Marquand fervently.

Chunky leaped to the opening, swung his sombrero as he leaned out, and uttered a long, shrill "y-e-o-w!"

A bullet chipped the adobe at his side. Stacy ducked, throwing himself on the floor, sucking a thumb energetically.

"Wing you?" inquired Kris Kringle.

"Somebody burned my thumb," wailed the fat boy.

"It was a bullet that burned you. Served you right too. Somebody tie that boy up or he'll be killed," counseled the guide.

The besiegers could not have failed to hear the shot from Tad's rifle, but it did not seem to disturb them. They evidently did not even dream that one of the party had escaped their vigilance and that he was well on his way for assistance.

The wait from that time on was a tedious and trying one, though each felt a certain sense of elation that Tad Butler had succeeded in outwitting the enemy.

It was shortly after two o'clock in the morning when Kris Kringle espied a party of horsemen slowly encircling the adobe house. The riders were strung out far off on the plain. Those hiding in the sage in front of the house could not see the approaching horsemen.

"There they come," whispered Kris Kringle. "Begin shooting!"

The two men started firing, while the besiegers poured volley after volley through the window.

The posse at this, closed in at a gallop. Their rifles now began to crash.

In a few minutes it was all over. The sheriff's men surrounded the besiegers, placing every man of them under arrest. After this the officers quickly liberated the Pony Rider Boys. Three of the besiegers had been wounded. Among them, was the Mexican whom Tad had defeated in the tilting game a few days before.

When all was over, the boys hoisted Tad Butler on their shoulders and marched around the adobe house shouting and singing. Mr. Marquand decided to go back with the posse, using these men as a guard for his treasure. It was understood that the Pony Rider Boys were to follow the next morning. Before leaving, Mr. Marquand called the Professor aside.

"There is, on a rough estimate, all of sixty thousand dollars in the treasure chest. Had it not been for you and your brave boys I should have lost it. So, when you reach Hondo to-morrow, I shall take great pleasure in presenting to each of you a draft for two thousand dollars."

Professor Zepplin protested, but Mr. Marquand insisted, and he kept his word. After the posse, with their prisoners and the treasure, had started, the Pony Rider Boys, arm in arm, started off across the moonlit meadows toward their camp. It was their last night in camp. Their summer's journeyings had come to an end—a fitting close to their adventurous travels. Not a word did they speak until they reached the camp. There, they turned and gazed off over the plain which was all silvered under the now clear light of the moon.

"It has been a silver trail," mused Tad Butler.

"It has indeed," breathed his companions

"And we've reached the end of The Silver Trail," added the Professor, coming up at that moment. "To-morrow I'll breathe the first free breath that I've drawn in three months."

The boys circled slowly around him and joined hands. Then their voices rose on the mellow desert air to the tune of

"Home, Sweet Home."

A week later saw the wanderers back in Chillicothe. Their welcome was a warm one. Banker Perkins found his once ailing son now transformed into a sturdy young giant.

We shall meet them again in the next volume of this series—in a tale of surpassing wonders—published under the title: "THE PONY RIDER BOYS IN THE GRAND CANYON; Or, the Mystery of Bright Angel Gulch." It will be found to be by far the most interesting volume so far published about the splendid Pony Rider Boys.

The End.